R.

*A*

### *Alarm rose in Taylor's eyes. "What are you up to?"*

"No good," Zelda replied cheerfully. "Isn't that what you expect of me?"

He backed into the counter. Zelda kept coming until her body was pressed against his, toe to toe, thigh to thigh, hips to . . . well, there was no doubt at all about what impact she was having on him.

"Zelda, what do you think you're doing?" he demanded in a choked whisper.

She noticed with a measure of satisfaction that, for all his protests, Taylor wasn't trying very hard to escape. "If you don't know, then you've been out of circulation far too long."

He wasn't nearly as immune as he'd pretended to be. Unfortunately, neither was she. So this game of hers could have dangerous consequences . . . .

But since when had that ever stopped her?

D.H.

Dear Reader,

Welcome to Silhouette *Special Edition*... welcome to romance.

Last year I requested your opinions on the books that we publish. Thank you for the many thoughtful comments. Throughout the past months I've been sharing quotes from these letters with you. This seems very appropriate while we are in the midst of our THAT SPECIAL WOMAN! promotion, as each of our readers is a very special woman.

This month, our THAT SPECIAL WOMAN! is Lt. Callie Donovan, a woman whose military career is on the line. Lindsay McKenna brings you this story of determination and love in *Point of Departure*.

Also this month is *Forever* by Ginna Gray, another book in the BLAINES AND THE McCALLS OF CROCKETT, TEXAS series. Erica Spindler brings you *Magnolia Dawn*, the second book in her BLOSSOMS OF THE SOUTH series. And don't miss Sherryl Woods's *A Daring Vow*— a tie-in to her VOWS series—as well as stories from Andrea Edwards and Jean Ann Donathan.

I hope you enjoy this book, and all of the stories to come!

Sincerely,

Tara Gavin
Senior Editor

QUOTE OF THE MONTH:

"I have an MA in Humanities. I like to read funny and spirited stories. I really enjoy novels set in distinctive parts of the country with strong women and equally strong men.... Please continue to publish books that are delightful to read. Nothing is as much fun as finding a great story. I will continue to buy books that entertain and make me smile."

—T. Kanowith, Maryland

# SHERRYL WOODS

## A DARING VOW

*Silhouette*®

SPECIAL EDITION®

Published by Silhouette Books

America's Publisher of Contemporary Romance

SILHOUETTE BOOKS

ISBN 0-373-09855-3

A DARING VOW

**Books by Sherryl Woods**

Silhouette Special Edition

*Safe Harbor* #425
*Never Let Go* #446
*Edge of Forever* #484
*In Too Deep* #522
*Miss Liz's Passion* #573
*Tea and Destiny* #595
*My Dearest Cal* #669
*Joshua and the Cowgirl* #713
*\*Love* #769
*\*Honor* #775
*\*Cherish* #781
*\*Kate's Vow* #824
*\*A Daring Vow* #855

*\*Vows

Silhouette Desire

*Not at Eight, Darling* #309
*Yesterday's Love* #329
*Come Fly with Me* #345
*A Gift of Love* #375
*Can't Say No* #431
*Heartland* #472
*One Touch of Moondust* #521
*Next Time...Forever* #601
*Fever Pitch* #620
*Dream Mender* #708

Silhouette Books

*Silhouette Summer Sizzlers* 1990
"A Bridge to Dreams"

---

## SHERRYL WOODS

lives by the ocean, which, she says, provides daily inspiration for the romance in her soul. She further explains that her years as a television critic taught her about steamy plots and humor; her years as a travel editor took her to exotic locations; and her years as a crummy weekend tennis player taught her to stick with what she enjoyed most—writing. "What better way is there," Sherryl asks, "to combine all that experience than by creating romantic stories?"

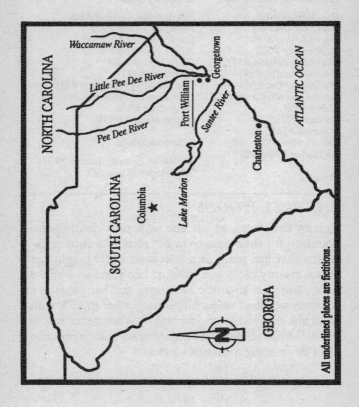

NORTH CAROLINA

*Waccamaw River*

*Little Pee Dee River*

*Pee Dee River*

Georgetown

Port William

Santee River

ATLANTIC OCEAN

Charleston

SOUTH CAROLINA

Columbia

*Lake Marion*

GEORGIA

N

All underlined places are fictitious.

## Prologue

With all the uncertainties in his life—and there were a bundle of them, one thing was absolutely, positively clear to Taylor Matthews. He did not want to handle the estate of Ella Louise Lane. Not under any circumstances.

In the first place, the woman was nuttier than a pecan pie. No medical examination had labeled her as such, but there were some things everyone in Port William, South Carolina, just accepted. Ella Louise's eccentricity was one of them.

In the second and far more bothersome place, her primary heir was likely to be her daughter. As Taylor recalled all too explicitly, Zelda Lane was sexier than Julia Roberts and more trouble than half a dozen bank robbers. He wasn't sure which side of her nature worried him more.

Unfortunately, Ella Louise had made up her mind she wanted Taylor for the job. She paced in front of him now wearing a bright orange sweater that clashed dramatically with her red hair, a faded pair of blue jeans that bagged on her too thin body and some kind of feathery, pink high-heeled slippers from another era. Mules, wasn't that what they called them? How could she even stand up on the things? he wondered nervously as she teetered dangerously, then sank onto the sofa. He breathed a sigh of relief.

"Have you got that?" she demanded.

He blinked and stared at her.

"Got what?" he asked, still too bemused by her command invitation and unwanted memories of Zelda to pay much attention to the details of a will he had no intention of drawing up.

The only reason he was in this house at all was out of some misguided sense of duty. He knew deep in his gut that he'd bungled things with Zelda and he owed her for it. But not this much. Uh-uh. Definitely not enough to get within five hundred miles of her again. His days of risk-taking had ended. He had a nice, quiet, ordinary life now, and that was the way he wanted things to stay. There was nothing quiet or ordinary about Zelda.

Ella Louise scowled at him, while tapping her foot impatiently. "I declare, Taylor, for a bright young attorney, you don't have a lick of concentration. Sometimes I wonder what my daughter ever saw in you."

She studied him critically, then shook her head in bafflement. Taylor winced at the assessment that had obviously found him wanting. He felt an odd need to defend himself, to prove his desirability by listing the attractive, intelligent, socially acceptable women who'd tried to seduce him since the death of his wife. Fortunately he was able to keep his mouth clamped firmly shut.

Obviously the reference to Zelda and their long-dead relationship was making him a little crazy, stirring him in a way it had no business doing. With that in mind he tried one more time to make Ella Louise see sense. He figured he was wasting his time, given the fact that he was dealing with a woman who'd made a shrine out of her collection of F. Scott Fitzgerald novels, while the rest of the house practically collapsed around her. Still he had to try.

"I really think you should hire another lawyer," he said. "I'll be glad to call over to Charleston and have a friend of mine stop by to see you."

"And how long will that take?" Ella Louise demanded. "Days? A week or two? I don't have time. I want this done and done now."

He regarded her even more nervously, studying the pale complexion and the feverish look in her eyes that he'd attributed to too many glasses of her favorite bourbon on an empty stomach. Was she suffering from some fatal illness, after all?

"Ella Louise," he inquired worriedly, "are you all right? Should I call the doctor?"

"So he can tell me I'm dying?" she said with an unladylike snort. "Don't need to hear him say it. I just need to get this one piece of business taken care of, so I can finally rest. Now can we get down to business or are you going to waste more of my time arguing?"

"You know Zelda and I didn't part on the best of terms," he protested in what had to be the biggest understatement since the local paper had described his political downfall as being the result of a slight mistake in judgment.

"I know," she agreed with such great serenity that Taylor was sure she couldn't possibly remember the details as vividly as he did. She must have forgotten all about the way Zelda had poked holes in every one of his brand new Mustang's tires the night he'd broken up with her. Then she'd painted an unwarranted comment about his parentage on the town's water tower. How she'd gotten up there was beyond him, but she'd always had a knack for managing the impossible.

Since he'd known deep down that he was the one at fault, he'd been the one who'd climbed that damned tower to remove the graffiti before his daddy went to the sheriff to demand Zelda's arrest. A part of him, a part that remained untamed despite his father's best efforts, had admired her audacity. He doubted she'd changed. The Zelda he remembered was capable of carrying a grudge on into the next century.

Given all that, he found Ella Louise's enigmatic expression disturbing.

"How can you ask that she deal with me at a time when she'd be grieving?" He shook his head. "No, Ella Louise, this is a bad idea. I'll get someone else here this afternoon." He could call in a favor at his old law firm. They wouldn't want to come, but they'd respond to the plea of a desperate man. He figured that was a role he wouldn't have a bit of trouble playing convincingly.

"I want you," she said stubbornly, then began a fit of coughing that had her whole body shaking.

Panicked by the increasingly obvious signs of some unnamed illness, Taylor finally agreed to take down her last wishes and put them into a legal will.

"But I won't be the executor," he said flatly. "You'll have to think of someone else. There's no point in upsetting Zelda any more than necessary at such a time. What about Mabel or Elsie? She always got along with them, didn't she?"

"I'll think about it," she agreed.

Too quickly, it seemed to him, but he was willing to grasp at straws.

"Meantime," she said blithely, "just put your name in there, and we'll discuss it when you bring the papers back for me to sign."

Taylor saw the stubborn set to her chin and remembered it all too well from countless quarrels with Zelda. With a sigh of resignation, he stopped arguing and took notes. It troubled him more than he could say, however, that that serene, enigmatic look was back in Ella Louise's eyes when he left.

That night his own mother gave him a lecture on generosity of spirit, forgiveness and Christian charity. He wasn't exactly sure which parts of her eloquent speech were applicable to Ella Louise's situation, but he finally threw in the towel. Besides, as nutty as Ella Louise was, she'd probably have half a dozen executors named before she finally died. Come to think of it, she was probably stubborn enough to outlive them all.

The next day, after an endless night filled with memories of all the times he'd defied his parents and sneaked out to that old tumble-down house during high school and college, he pulled to a stop in the front yard. He could still recall as if it had been only yesterday the way Zelda had looked as she'd run down that dirt path from the front door, eyes sparkling with devilment, cheeks flushed with excitement, those long, long legs as bare as pure temptation. She'd had more spirit, more wild passion than any woman he'd ever known. The memory alone was enough to cause his body to grow hard with desire.

Let that be a warning, he thought ruefully as he tried to think of some way to extricate himself from the dangerous situation that Ella Louise's signature on that damned will would just about guarantee. It was a time bomb, just ticking away, setting him up for disaster.

He tapped on the screen door and peered into the dim interior. When Ella Louise didn't respond, he walked around the outside of the house looking for her, climbing over rusting wheelbarrows and haphazardly stacked piles of firewood. Filled with a sudden sense of impending doom, he returned to the front door, called out one last time, then crept inside.

He spotted her right off. Ella Louise was sitting in a rocker, her head slumped forward. Taylor knew without setting one foot closer that she was dead, that she'd finished up her earthly business with him the previous afternoon and died quietly in her sleep.

So, he thought with wry amusement, she'd gotten her wish, after all. Even without her signature, he knew he could make the will stick in court unless somebody wanted to raise a humdinger of a stink. Just as he'd feared, he was doomed to handling the settlement of Ella Louise's estate.

Which meant seeing Zelda again.

God help him.

## *Chapter One*

So, Zelda Lane thought as she slowly hung up the phone, her mother had finally gone and gotten her wish. She'd fallen asleep in her antique rocking chair and never awakened, according to the neighbor who'd just called.

As she tried to absorb the news, Zelda was torn between the predictable emptiness and a fierce anger that accompanied any loss. There was even an unwelcome touch of guilt mixed in. Her eyes stung but remained dry through a sheer act of will. She would not cry. She wouldn't even mourn. How could she shed so much as a tear over the death of a woman who'd been determined to kill herself as far back as Zelda could remember?

"Damn you, Mama," she whispered with a catch in her voice. "Damn you!"

Her boss regarded her with alarm. "Zelda, are you all right?" Kate Newton asked, coming around from behind her desk to squeeze Zelda's suddenly trembling hand.

Zelda glanced up, feeling dazed, and caught the expression of genuine concern in Kate's eyes. "It's Mama," she said flatly. "She died sometime during the night. She was at home, all alone, just the way she wanted it to happen."

Ready, sympathetic tears immediately sprang into Kate's eyes. "Oh, sweetie, I'm so sorry." Then as if it weren't the middle of an incredibly busy day, she said, "Come on. We'll shut down for the afternoon, and I'll help you pack."

"Pack?" Zelda said blankly, clutching her steno pad more tightly. "For what?"

"I'm sure you'll want to be on the first flight back east. Don't you worry about a thing. I'll call the airlines and take care of the reservations."

Zelda shook her head. "No." Her voice held steady with no sign of the turmoil she was feeling inside. She pretended not to see the look of puzzlement in Kate's eyes as she stubbornly opened her pad to a clean page. "You were about to dictate a letter when I got that call."

Dismay spread across Kate's face. Zelda stared her down. After a moment's hesitation, Kate swallowed whatever lecture she'd been about to begin and finished dictating. But before Zelda could escape to the outer office, Kate gently removed the pad from her hand, a glint of determination in her eyes. When it came to stubbornness, they were an equal match.

"Zelda, I know you must be in shock, but denying what's happened won't help," she said gently.

"I'm not denying anything," Zelda contradicted. "My mother's dead. She finally got her wish. She's been trying to kill herself with booze and cigarettes ever since I can remember."

A wayward tear escaped despite her stoic determination not to admit how much that hurt. Before Kate could ask more troubling questions, Zelda ran from the office. By the time Kate caught up with her, she was already at her computer typing the letter her boss had just dictated. The keystrokes were automatic, though she had to force herself to concentrate on the shorthand that seemed shakier and less precise than usual. Kate finally sighed and gently closed the door between their offices in an attempt to give her the privacy she desperately wanted to avoid.

Her keystrokes finally slowed. Memories forced their way in, more powerful than the determination to avoid them. *Oh, Mama,* she thought wearily. *How could you slip away on me like this?* She asked the question, but she already knew the answer. Her mother had slipped away on her and everyone else years ago.

Everybody in Port William, South Carolina, always knew that Zelda Lane's mama was "under the weather" by three o'clock in the afternoon. Except on weekends, that is. Saturdays and Sundays, when Zelda's daddy was home, Ella Louise started drinking earlier and reached her limit well before noon. It was a well-established pattern that never varied, even when Zelda begged her mother not to touch another drink.

After Joseph Lane died at the age of thirty-eight in a boating accident, Ella Louise no longer wasted time sipping mint juleps in the way of old-fashioned, genteel Southern ladies. She switched to bourbon, taking it smooth and neat, from a coffee mug that appropriately enough said Life's A Bitch...And Then You Die.

Though she loved her mother fiercely, Zelda found Ella Louise to be an embarrassment, especially when she wandered into town and caused such a commotion in the local bar that Sheriff Wiley had to drive her home. It had happened so regularly that people finally stopped commenting on it. They just shook their heads and viewed little Zelda with the sympathy they'd bestow on anyone in her sorry plight.

Refusing to allow her embarrassment to show, Zelda had learned at an early age to poke that stubborn chin of hers into the air and thumb her nose at their condescension. She had a temper to match her fiery red hair and one way or another she'd been telling the whole miserable town of Port William to take a hike practically since the day she was born. It was a skill her mama had instilled in her after years of perfecting it herself.

It had been ten years since Zelda had left Port William far behind to make a new home for herself in Los Angeles. She'd begged her mother to come with her at first, then resigned herself to the fact that Ella Louise would never leave the town where she'd been raised. She'd been determined to die in that decrepit house where she'd lived her whole pitiful life. She'd been a martyr to the bitter end, as far as Zelda could see.

"My life's over, honey. You grab what you can," she'd said more than once.

And so, with only minimal reluctance, Zelda had. She'd put her wild days behind her and settled down, content in the knowledge that no one in Los Angeles knew a thing about her background. She'd fooled her friends into thinking she was just any other normal woman with hopes and dreams and the determination to attain them. None of them realized exactly how driven she was to escape her past.

Now it seemed that past was about to catch up with her.

Though she couldn't avoid Kate's worried looks, Zelda did manage to get through an entire week without having to answer any more questions about her mother or about Port William. Furious with herself for the sign of weakness, she shed her tears late at night. In those dark, lonely hours, she tried desperately not to regret the fact that she hadn't been back home once in all the years since she'd left. She couldn't see much point in going now, when the only person in the entire town she'd ever loved was gone. Already buried, in fact, thanks to the instructions she'd given.

A fleeting image of Taylor Matthews crossed her mind and then was banished. Strong, gentle, wicked Taylor, she thought with a reluctant sigh. Okay, maybe there was one other person in Port William that she had loved, but those glorious days and wild nights were best forgotten. Taylor certainly hadn't been able to put them behind him fast enough, she recalled with a bitterness that time had done nothing to mellow.

The phone rang and as if her thoughts alone had conjured him up, she heard Taylor's voice. She recognized it at once, though it was deeper now, even sexier, which somehow infuriated her. She couldn't quite decide, though, whether it was him she was mad at or herself for responding to that husky and no doubt unintended sensuality.

"Yes," she said coolly, when she could finally catch her breath.

He cleared his throat. "Zelda, I'm real sorry about your mother."

"Thank you," she said stiffly, surprised that he would bother making a condolence call.

"Look, I don't know if your mother told you what she had in mind, but I saw her the day before she died."

"Why on earth would you go see Mama?"

"She asked me to come."

"She asked you to come," she repeated with undisguised astonishment.

"Yes. Actually, well, the bottom line is that I'm handling the estate."

"You're what?" *Oh, Mama, what the hell have you gone and done?* Zelda thought with a mounting sense of desperation. Determined not to let Taylor hear even one tiny hint of her dismay, she steadied her voice. "Fine, Taylor. Do whatever Mama wanted."

"It's not quite that simple." He sighed heavily, sounding more put-upon than Beau Matthews ever had when he'd been lecturing Taylor on his many indiscretions, most of which he attributed directly to his son's association with Zelda. "Actually, it's damned complicated. I think you'd better come home so we can discuss it."

"That's not possible," she said without hesitation. "You're the lawyer, the executor, whatever. You deal with it."

"Look," he said with a trace of impatience, "there is nothing I would like better than to close things up and send you a check, but it's not that easy. There are decisions to be made, and they have to be made by you. You'll have to come home."

Being told what she had to do, especially by Taylor, only strengthened her resolve. "No."

"Why, Zelda?" he said, his voice gentling for the first time. "You afraid to come back here, sugar?"

With a sinking sensation in the pit of her stomach, she heard the familiar dare in his tone. He'd gotten her into trees, onto rooftops, into trouble with those taunting dares of his. *Sugar,* hell!

"I'm not afraid of anything, Taylor Matthews," she snapped, falling into a trap as old as the first day they'd met. She heard his low, satisfied chuckle and bit off a few more choice words that occurred to her. Finally she gave in to the inevitable. "Okay," she said grudgingly. "I'll do what I can."

"Soon, Zelda."

Was he anxious to see her? More likely, just anxious to get it over with. "I'll be there when I get there," she told him with her very last bit of spunk.

She slammed the phone down then because she couldn't tolerate one more smug word, one tiny little hint of I-told-you-so in his voice. Then she sat staring at the phone, dismayed. She was going home. She would see Taylor again. Dear Lord, what had she been thinking of? What had her mother been thinking of to get her into this mess?

The fact that Ella Louise had left an estate tangled in so much red tape that Zelda had no choice but to go back to Port William to straighten it out didn't particularly surprise her. Her mother never had been one for doing things the ordinary way. It was Taylor's involvement that was a kick-in-the-pants shock.

Still stunned, she went in to explain to Kate that she needed time off, after all.

"Of course, you have to go," Kate said at once, her expression clearly relieved that Zelda had finally seen sense. "Take as much time as you need. I'll call in that temp we used on your last vacation. If there's anything I can do for you from here to straighten things out, if you need legal advice, you just have to call."

Zelda fiddled with the back of the chair she'd been clutching for support. "I hate leaving you in the lurch, though. You have that big divorce case coming up next week. Maybe I should put this trip off. It's not as if I can do anything for Mama now. Besides, how much of an estate can there be? Last I checked, she was dirt poor and wouldn't take a dime from me to change that. Maybe I ought to let the state take her pitiful possessions and get on with my life."

Kate's gaze narrowed at the suggestion. Zelda knew her brilliant legal mind was bound to consider such an idea practically sacrilegious.

"Zelda, is there some reason you don't want to go back to South Carolina?"

Zelda couldn't figure out how to explain that she hadn't been able to leave Port William fast enough. She was a different person now, confident, respected ... tamed, some might say. She didn't want to alter Kate's impression of her, but she could see from her boss's determined expression that nothing but the truth would end the cross-examination. As a whole slew of opposing attorneys knew, Kate was a master of the technique.

"You know how you see those shows about slow, backwater towns and you think they're just old-fashioned stereotypes?" Zelda said eventually. "Well, Port William is the prototype. The people there didn't know exactly what to make of Mama, and they certainly didn't know what to make of me. She named me after F. Scott Fitzgerald's loony wife, for goodness' sake. All the townspeople knew about Fitzgerald was what they'd figured out from reading *The Great Gatsby.* It didn't leave a great impression in their narrow little minds."

"Surely they didn't blame you for being named for some dead author's crazy wife?"

"Blame me?" Zelda replied thoughtfully. "I don't suppose so. They just figured I was destined to follow the same path into a mental institution or else live out my days like Mama in some drunken stupor. And that was before I moved to Los Angeles. Now they'll probably want to hold an exorcism to rid me of the devil."

Kate, born and raised in trend-setting, accepting L.A., looked skeptical. "It can't be that bad."

Zelda didn't argue, but she knew in her heart that she'd actually given the town the benefit of the doubt. The sheriff was probably painting up a cell just for her return. Folks in Port William had never entirely understood that the things she'd done had been the high-spirited hijinks of a teenager trying desperately to live up to the failed dreams of a sad and lost mother. If she could have splashed in public fountains at midnight, as her namesake reportedly had, she would have done it. Port William, however, had been short on fountains. It was probably just as well. She'd gotten into enough mischief as it was.

She'd been easy prey for a boy such as Taylor, who'd had his own demons to sort through and had known just how to tease her into accompanying him. Foolishly, she'd thought that their daring exploits would bond them together forever, but she couldn't have been more wrong. In the end, Taylor had proved himself to be every bit a Matthews—disgustingly stuffy, terrifyingly ambitious and thoroughly predictable. He had rid himself of the wild girl from the wrong side of the tracks without a backward glance.

She'd hated him for abandoning her, for leaving her lost and alone in a town that could never understand her longing for acceptance. Even more, though, she had hated seeing the passionate man she'd loved since childhood become another sacrifice to the Matthews tradition. She wondered if he'd turned out to be every bit as stodgy as his father, or if some spark of that individuality and spunk he'd shown with her had remained.

No use speculating, she thought. She'd find out soon enough. To her deep regret, her pulse bucked a little just at the prospect.

She was going to see Taylor Matthews again.

God help her.

## Chapter Two

Port William looked exactly as Zelda had remembered it, exactly as it had looked for the past century, probably. Pine trees littered the ground with their long, slippery needles. With the exception of one or two sadly neglected plantation houses on the outskirts of town and the big, brick Matthews place on top of a hill overlooking the river, most of the community consisted of small clapboard houses. Almost without exception, each had a wide front porch, a rocking chair or swing from which to observe the passing of time, and a row of azalea bushes turning brown as the chill air of autumn belligerently pushed its way south. The lazy Waccamaw River wound its way toward the sea, providing a few picturesque settings in the lowland locale that was an otherwise quaint painting that time had faded.

As she drove in from Charleston, her speed slowing with every mile, Zelda made note of the few obvious changes, starting with the familiar welcome sign that announced that the town of Port William, founded in 1756, now boasted a population of 1,027. It had grown.

Beyond that, the only real concession to the nineties that she could see was a strip mall about two miles from the center of town. It consisted of a national discount store, a modern grocery store and a video rental store. On the outside, at least, everything else looked almost the same, except for a new coat of paint here and there and some visible updating of equipment.

Based on the number of pickups jammed along the strip of asphalt in front, Harlan's Feed and Grain was still the gathering place for men, a handful of tobacco growers and the usually out-of-work textile mill employees. The fancy riding mowers displayed on the back side of the parking lot, however, suggested Harlan had updated his stock to more high-tech, high-priced wonders. She couldn't imagine who was buying them.

Vera Mae's Salon de Beauty had new curtains hanging on the windows, but through the open doorway Zelda could see the same old red-vinyl chairs inside. She wondered if Vera Mae was still doing her famous beehive hairdos and cementing them in place with spray.

Next door, Sarah Lynn's Diner was packed with the lunch crowd. Zelda was willing to bet Monday was still the day Sarah Lynn baked her famous lemon meringue pie. She doubted the plump, matronly woman, who'd looked after Zelda like one of her own, had gone trendy and put key lime pie on the menu in its place. The locals would shun such innovation, dismissing it as putting on airs.

Zelda ignored the fact that her mouth was watering at the thought of that lemon meringue pie. She wasn't up to announcing her presence in town quite yet, much less handling Sarah Lynn's sympathy. Instead she drove her rental car straight on to the house in which she'd grown up.

When she pulled onto the tiny patch of lawn, she turned off the engine and sat staring at the old frame house, which was badly in need of paint. It was no better or worse than most of the houses around it, but Zelda had always resented the way her parents had let it go to seed. When she was fifteen, she'd earned enough money to buy paint and had given it a coat of white herself, slapping it on with zeal, if not neatness. From the looks of it, that was the last coat of paint it had received.

Not quite ready to go inside, she rolled down the car window and drew in a lungful of the fresh, pine-scented air. Memories crowded in like so many teenagers trying to be first in line for concert tickets. A few of those memories were even good, like the time she and Jimmy Martin had sat on the creaky front porch swing holding hands while Mama played Grandpa's old Glenn Miller records inside. And there was the time Taylor Matthews had pelted her bedroom window with stones in the middle of the night and dared her to go skinny-dipping in the river with him. Naturally, she hadn't been able to resist.

Taylor Matthews, she thought with yet another sigh. He figured in too many memories of her past. To her disgust, ever since his call, she hadn't been able to get him out of her mind. Once they'd been drawn together as inevitably as any two star-crossed lovers in history. In the end, though, it had all turned to ashes.

Damn his father's political ambitions! she thought with as much vehemence now as she had then. If it hadn't been for Beau Matthews's obsessive drive to see his boy in the state capitol—or the White House, for that matter—she could have claimed Taylor's heart publicly. Everyone in town saw that he was sweet on her, anyway.

But once Taylor had passed adolescence and started listening to his father, he'd begun hating himself for those wicked, wayward feelings he couldn't control. She had seen it in his eyes and slowly withdrew into a protective shell, determined that he would never see how his change in attitude was quietly killing her. She'd had one lapse, the night he'd finally broken up with her, and to this day she regretted letting him know how much his defection had mattered.

She couldn't help wondering now if he'd finally found some suitable, boring woman to stand by his side and satisfy his daddy's standards. In all the years she'd been away from Port William, she had never asked about Taylor and her mother had never volunteered a word. It was just as well. Zelda hated being wrong, and she'd never in her life been more wrong than she had been about Taylor. He might have been sexy as sin and he might have exhibited exactly the kind of dangerous, wild streak that appealed to her in his teens, but he'd grown up into a stuffy, judgmental man—just like her own daddy, who'd trampled on Ella Louise's spirit until she was nothing more than a shadowy presence.

That, she thought, snapping herself back to the present, was a whole other kettle of fish. And one she didn't intend to explore, not today, not ever if she could help it.

The Port William grapevine was apparently still in fine working order. Within minutes of her arrival, Zelda was surrounded by a group of neighbors, all wearing black and all bearing covered dishes. She'd be eating macaroni and cheese, green bean casseroles and Jell-O salads for a month.

"Why on earth did Mama ask Taylor to handle her estate?" Zelda asked the three women in order to cut off their insincere murmurs of sympathy. Not one of them had said a kind word about her mother when she was alive. Still, Zelda credited them with having more insight into her mama's final days than she did. "Did she explain that to any of you?"

"Well, he is a lawyer, honey," Mabel Smith reminded her.

Zelda caught Mabel trying to keep her disapproving gaze off of Zelda's colorful outfit, a thrift-shop ensemble of gauzy, floating materials that bore her own unmistakable flair for the dramatic. No doubt Mabel considered it totally unsuitable for mourning. Zelda knew, however, that her mother would have loved it. In fact, she could probably find some floppy picture hat to match hidden away in the back of her mother's closet.

"Taylor's the only lawyer in town these days, come to think of it," Betty Sue Conner chimed in.

"What happened to Will Rutledge?" Zelda asked, recalling the sweet old man whose office had always reeked of pipe smoke.

"Dead."

"John Tatum?" She tried to keep the note of desperation out of her voice. Surely she could hire someone else to represent her to deal with Taylor.

"Moved to Charleston, five, maybe six years ago," Mabel said.

"Honey, I thought you and Taylor were friends once upon a time. More than that, in fact," Elsie Whittingham said. "Why I can recall plain as day the time that old man Highsmith found the two of you up in his hayloft. What a ruckus that caused!''

Betty Sue grinned. ''Almost gave Beau Matthews a heart attack. He thought sure you'd end up pregnant and ruin all his big plans for Taylor.'' Her expression suddenly sobered. ''Funny how things turn out, isn't it?''

''Betty Sue,'' Mabel said in a low voice clearly meant to shush her.

Zelda let the warning go by, too lost in memories to question either one of them about it. Why wouldn't those memories—good and bad—wither and die the way they should? Ten years should have been enough time to rob them of any impact at all. Obviously she didn't have a lick of willpower.

She tried harder to put them aside, but she couldn't seem to help recalling in explicit detail the way she'd felt being held in Taylor's arms up in that hayloft, or the surge of adrenaline she'd felt scrambling down and running away when they'd been caught. Their laughter had echoed on the night air, along with old man Highsmith's shouts and the sound of a shotgun being fired into the sky as a warning. She'd never run so fast in her life, clinging to Taylor's hand all the way, knowing that whatever happened they were in it together.

Despite the danger—or perhaps because of it—it had been one of the happiest moments of her life. This wasn't the first time it had come back to haunt her. No man had ever made her feel as exciting and alive as she had that night. The comparisons, whether she liked admitting it or not, were what had kept her single.

But she was a different woman now, and Taylor most assuredly was a different man. That was what she had to keep reminding herself as she tried to block those old feelings.

Before she could satisfactorily push the memory aside, however, the screen door squeaked and the man in question stood before her, bathed in the last rays of fading sunlight. Leave it to Taylor to make an unforgettable entrance. A TV evangelist couldn't have asked for a more dramatic backdrop.

Taylor stood where he was, hands shoved in his pockets, and nodded. "Zelda."

Since one word was all he seemed able to manage, Zelda matched him. "Taylor."

The three fluttering female guests suddenly thought of a dozen excuses for why they had to rush home. During their whirlwind departure, Zelda tried to gather her composure. She figured the best she could hope for was the restraint to keep from throwing herself right smack into Taylor's muscular arms. Why the devil couldn't the man have gone all soft? Maybe even bald? Instead, he was as lean and handsome as ever.

She couldn't seem to stop herself from drinking in the sight of him, from the fancy suit that couldn't hide his football-broad shoulders to the untamed curl in his jet black hair, from the combative angle of his jaw to the spark of defiance in his clear gray eyes. That spark was a dead giveaway that Taylor hadn't changed, after all. He was already just daring her to do something outrageous, something he could no doubt condemn her for afterward. This time, though, she wouldn't give him the satisfaction. She'd outgrown the need to defy the world at every turn. She would be pleasant, calm, mature...even if it killed her.

She rose to her full height, an impressive five foot nine, and said in her most gracious but distant tone, "May I offer you a cup of tea?"

Taylor blinked, then looked startled by the sight of her mother's treasured silver teapot sitting on the scarred coffee table amid a collection of mismatched but elegant china cups. From the thunderstruck expression on his face, it was clear he hadn't expected her to know the first thing about the social amenities. Zelda could have told him that no female could grow up in the South without learning a thing or two about social graces, whether they ever practiced them or not. Maybe he'd just figured to find her drinking the last of her mama's bourbon.

"I suppose," he said finally.

To her amusement he sounded as if he didn't quite trust her ability to brew a drinkable pot of tea. Or perhaps he wasn't sure even after all this time that she wouldn't lace it with arsenic. Admittedly, the thought did hold a certain appeal.

"I'll taste mine first, if that'll put your mind at ease," she said wryly, causing him to scowl as an embarrassed flush crept up his neck.

When they each had a cup and she'd taken a healthy swallow, she deliberately cast a defiant look in his direction. He regarded her warily. For a man who'd once displayed a remarkably silver-tongued charm, he seemed at a loss for words. She wasn't inclined to help him out. She had enough to do just to keep her cup from rattling in its saucer and betraying her nerves.

"I'm sorry about your mother," he said eventually.

He'd said it before on the phone. She hadn't believed it then, either. Still, she nodded politely, thinking that he had a lot more to feel sorry about. Though Zelda doubted that she'd hear an apology for any of his past transgressions, she waited just the same.

During the gap in the conversation, she filled the time by checking out the status of his ring finger, mad at herself for caring, and trying not to be too obvious about it. No wedding band, she saw with some astonishment. And Taylor was definitely the type who'd want a ring to show the world that he was a family man and therefore suitably settled down and capable of handling the responsibilities of public office. The discovery kept her speechless. It also triggered an alarm, warning her to keep her guard up. A married Taylor would have been beyond reach. An unmarried Taylor spelled danger in capital letters.

Taylor finally broke the silence. "I'm glad you could come home."

"You insisted," she reminded him.

"True. As I explained on the phone, I'm afraid your mother's will is somewhat unorthodox," he said as if that were no less than anyone might have expected of Ella Louise. A nervous smile tugged at his lips, then disappeared under her disapproving gaze.

Because that hesitant smile reminded her of the boy who'd stolen her heart, it played havoc with Zelda's insides. It wasn't a reaction she was wild about. To keep things businesslike and on track, she said hurriedly, "What's so strange about it?"

Taylor leaned forward, his elbows propped on his knees. That posture could make a woman believe she had his full attention, that she was the most important thing in his universe. She wondered how many women, besides her, it had fooled.

"On the surface," he said, "the will seems pretty straightforward. You're her only heir. This house belongs to you now, along with some cash, some nice shares of several blue chips she'd bought years ago and, of course, all of her personal possessions."

Though it was considerably more than Zelda had expected, the details didn't sound complicated to her. She regarded him in confusion. "What's so odd about that?"

"Nothing," he admitted. "However, there is a condition."

Zelda's pulse skipped a beat. "Which is?" she asked with an increasingly familiar sense of dread. What crazy notion had Ella Louise gotten into her head in those final months? She stared nervously at Taylor and waited.

He met her gaze and a flicker of some long-forgotten emotion rose in his eyes. He cleared his throat, tugged at his already loosened tie, blinked and looked away. Finally he said, "She wants you to live in the house for one year."

Zelda could feel the panic building inside. She glanced around the dreary room with its tattered wallpaper of fading cabbage roses, dusty drapes and uncomfortable furniture, and felt as if she'd just been sentenced to prison. Why on earth would her mother ask such a thing? Even though she hadn't had the gumption to act on it, Zelda knew that Ella Louise had longed all her life to be away from here.

"And if I don't?"

"It all goes to establish a scholarship for a writer, the F. Scott Fitzgerald Memorial Scholarship, to be exact. You'll get nothing except her collection of books. They are first editions, by the way."

Zelda held back a desire to moan. It wasn't that she wanted the property, the handful of stocks or the paltry amount of cash. Kate paid her well and she was happy in Los Angeles without any of that. But this place, this hated place, was her mama's only legacy. How could she walk away from that as if it didn't matter? How could she ignore her mama's last wish, no matter how bizarre, no matter how it might turn her life upside down?

"There is no way around this crazy stipulation?"

"None. I drew it up myself. It's airtight."

Taylor sounded almost regretful about that, she noted, wondering if he hoped she'd try to break the will, anyway. Maybe Kate could find a loophole, she thought with a flash of hope. She dismissed the idea almost as readily as it had come to her. She couldn't even consider such an action unless she understood what had been in her mother's mind when she drew up the document.

"How long ago did she make out this will?" she asked.

"The day she called me to the house, the day before she died."

"So recently?" she said in amazement. "Was there any question . . . ? Could she have been confused?"

"You know how Ella Louise was," he said dryly. "But I'd have to say her mind was clear as a bell. She knew exactly what she wanted. Knowing how you'd feel about it, I even tried to argue with her about naming me executor, but she was determined. She wouldn't hear of asking someone else to do it."

"Why was it so important to her that I come home? Did she tell you that?"

Apparently he heard the dismay in her voice. For the first time since he'd walked into the house, Taylor regarded her with real sympathy. "She said that deep down you were two of a kind, that eventually you'd figure it out."

"Cryptic to the end," Zelda said, because she absolutely refused to say what she was really thinking, that despite Taylor's impression otherwise, her mother had finally lost her always fragile grip on reality like one of those pathetic, dreamy southern heroines Tennessee Williams wrote about so well.

His mission completed, Taylor rose with an obvious expression of relief. "What will you do?"

Zelda sighed. "I don't know," she said honestly. "I just don't know."

"Is there... Are you involved with someone in Los Angeles? Do you need to get back?"

She couldn't tell from looking at him how he might feel about it if there was a man waiting for her. Pride made her want to invent the hottest romance on record. But even as the words of the lie formed on her lips, she was already shaking her head.

"A career?" he asked. "You've been out there a long time now. It must seem like home."

"It does. I have friends. I have a wonderful job. I'd hate to leave it," she admitted, but she knew that Kate would probably grant her a leave of absence to do whatever she had to do. In the past few months, since her own marriage, Kate had placed a whole new emphasis on the meaning of family.

Zelda looked directly at Taylor, into eyes that had once gazed on her with so much love and tenderness. Were any of those old emotions left at all? Did she even want there to be? Because she'd once respected his opinion, once believed he knew her even better than she had known herself, she asked, "What do you think I should do? Should I fight this? Should I give everything up? Or should I stay here and make the best of it?"

She wasn't sure what she hoped to hear him say in response to that—that he'd missed her, that he wanted her back in Port William for his own selfish reasons. Naturally, though, those were not the words that crossed his lips.

"I can't advise you on something this personal. You have to do what you think is best, Zelda," he said as if he'd rehearsed it a dozen times.

To her irritation, he'd refused to look her in the eye when he'd said it.

"That's right," she snapped, suddenly furious at his careful, noncommittal response. "It wouldn't do for you to have an opinion now, would it? Maybe I should just call Beau and ask him." She glared at Taylor, saw the immediate, angry glint in his eyes that told her she'd gone too far. "Oh, never mind. When do I have to decide?"

"There's no rush, but the sooner we get things rolling, the better, if you decide you want to sell."

She couldn't miss the hopeful note in his voice. She knew in that instant that Taylor Matthews wanted

her as far away from Port William as it was human-
ly possible for her to get.

Perversely, that was all it took to make her want to
stay.

## *Chapter Three*

Word spread faster than a brushfire that Zelda Lane was back in town. There was some subdued whooping and rejoicing over coffee at Sarah Lynn's the morning after her arrival, mostly from men who recalled her daredevil nature, flaming red hair and statuesque proportions. Some of them were the same men Taylor had once warned rather emphatically to steer clear of her.

Now he shook his head just listening to them. A part of him wished he could say what he was thinking and feeling so easily. Hell, he didn't even know exactly what he was feeling. Guilt was probably part of it, guilt over treating her so shabbily. Anger that he'd let her get away?

No, damn it. Anger would imply caring, and he refused to admit how much he'd cared and how foolishly he'd tossed it all aside. Besides, emotions were costly. He'd learned that the hard way. Emotions were something he hadn't allowed himself for a very long time.

He found himself wondering how Zelda would react to all the attention. For a woman who claimed to want her presence to go unnoticed, she certainly hadn't done much to assure it. That red convertible she'd rented stuck out like a sore thumb among the standard gray sedans and pickups of most of Port William's residents. Yet he couldn't help thinking it was typically Zelda, flashy, sexy as the dickens and definitely inappropriate for a woman in mourning. The general consensus around him seemed to be that Zelda probably hadn't changed one whit.

Taylor had to agree. The woman he'd seen the day before had been dressed with no regard to fashion sense or propriety. There might have been yards and yards of that orange and yellow fabric, but it had draped and clung in a way that had tantalized. Her earthy sensuality had simmered just below the surface, even as she sedately offered him some of that tepid tea. There'd been a defiant spark in those turquoise eyes of hers that offered up a ready challenge. And yet he'd sensed that under it all the vulnerability that had once touched his heart was still there. He'd also known that she would have denied it vehemently.

As he recalled his gut-level reaction to just being in the same room with her again, he caught the speculative glances cast in his direction. The conversation around him swirled on, with Zelda very much at the center of it. He felt as if battery acid were pitching in his stomach. Maybe it was no more than the caffeine he'd consumed during a long and restless night, but he doubted it. Chances were he could blame it all on seeing Zelda again.

He'd hoped—no, he'd prayed—that he'd be immune to her, that he'd walk into that house, take one look at her and wonder how she'd ever been able to tie him in knots. Instead his pulse had reacted as if she'd been buck naked and pleading for his touch, when all she'd done was stand there prim and proper and offer him tea. It just proved that time and common sense were no match for wayward hormones.

Oh, well, he'd done his duty, he consoled himself. There was no need for him to be in the same room with her again, at least not for longer than it took to sign a document or two. Despite the uncertainty she'd expressed, he'd been able to tell from her panicked expression and the desperate look she'd cast around that awful house that she would hightail it back to her exciting life in Los Angeles the first chance she got. Temptation would depart with her.

At that prospect, he uttered a heartfelt sigh of relief and finished his coffee. Before he could set down the cup, Sarah Lynn bustled over with a fresh pot.

"More, hon?"

Taylor shook his head. "I've got to get to the office."

Sarah Lynn didn't take the hint. She didn't even know the meaning of the phrase. She slid into the seat opposite him. "Not before you tell me all about Zelda," she said, clearly in the mood for a long chat. "I heard you were out at her house first thing."

"Because I'm handling her mother's will," he pointed out, not liking the way she seemed to have transformed his purely professional visit into something personal. If it hadn't been for that damned will, he wouldn't have been within a hundred miles of the Lane house, at least not with Zelda in it. Sarah Lynn ought to know that about as well as anyone. She'd been there for Zelda, when the girl had been spitting mad and hurt because Taylor'd walked out on her. She'd given him her two cents on the subject, listened to his pitiful explanation, then somehow managed to stay loyal to both of them.

"Don't try to turn my stopping by on her first day home into anything else," he warned.

Sarah Lynn looked unconvinced. Still, she kept her opinion of his defensiveness to herself. "Whatever," she said blandly. "How's she look?"

Before he could muster a disinterested reply, a knowing, delighted grin spread across Sarah Lynn's round face. "Never mind, I can see by the look in your eyes that she must be as gorgeous as ever. She still gets to you, huh?" she said, rubbing it in.

"You two were hotter than a bowl of five-star chili once upon a time. It's damn near impossible to put out that kind of a flame. I oughta know. I've never forgotten that gorgeous Texan who swooped through town and swept me off my feet forty years ago. Talk about fireworks! You and Zelda used to get that exact same look in your eyes when you'd spot each other and thought no one else was looking."

Taylor scowled at her but tried to keep his irritation out of his voice. It wouldn't do to overreact. It would just set more tongues wagging. "Sarah Lynn, honey," he teased, "has anyone ever told you you have an overly active imagination?"

"No one whose opinion I trust," she smart-mouthed back. "Why don't you bring her on by for lunch?"

At her assumption that he and Zelda would pick up right where they'd left off, his fragile hold on his patience snapped. "If Zelda wants to eat here, she knows the way," he reminded her irritably as he slid from the booth. "Frankly, I'm not all that sure she'll be around long enough."

Sarah Lynn chuckled, obviously putting her own interpretation on his sour attitude. "Bye-bye, hon. You have a good one, you hear."

Taylor doubted any day that had started out with one of Sarah Lynn's inquisitions about her silly, romantic imaginings could possibly turn out to be good. The walk down the block to the old clapboard house that served as both his home and his office was short enough to be uneventful, but also too short to improve his mood.

Inside the office, the normally effusive Darlene Maitland greeted him with a subdued expression. Darlene was twenty-two, recently married and could type with fervor, if not accuracy. She was the only person in town who'd applied for the job of secretary when he'd posted a notice on the bulletin board at Sarah Lynn's. Since she was known for her bubbling enthusiasm—she'd been head cheerleader every year in high school—Taylor had a feeling her downcast look did not bode well for the rest of his morning.

"Guess what?" she said, following him into his office and plunking a handful of pink message slips onto his desk.

"What?" he said, in no mood to play guessing games.

"I'm pregnant!"

He regarded her as if she'd just announced that a bomb had arrived in the morning mail. Obviously he could not voice his real reaction to the news. "Congratulations!" he said with what he hoped was enough sincerity to cover his dismay.

If Darlene sensed his lack of enthusiasm, she didn't show it. "Thanks," she said, practically bursting with excitement now that the news was out. "Tommy Ray and I weren't counting on this, but it'll be okay." She shook her head, her hand resting protectively on her still-flat stomach. "A baby! Can you imagine?"

"It's something, all right."

She regarded him more somberly. "It means I'm going to have to quit, though."

There it was, the bombshell he'd been waiting for. The pregnancy, with its prospects of morning sickness and time off for shopping and lunchtime showers couldn't possibly have been enough. Oh, no. Darlene had to go and quit, too. It just about clinched the day's status as one of the worst in his life.

"Quit? Why on earth would you want to do that?" he demanded, unable to keep the cranky note from his voice. What had happened to all those women who wanted to have careers and motherhood? Taylor wondered miserably. "When's the baby due, anyway?"

"Not for another six months, but Tommy Ray figures I ought to go ahead and quit now so we can work on building a nursery and getting it all fixed up. I won't leave you in the lurch or anything. I figured you ought to be able to find somebody to replace me in two weeks. I could start looking around for you right away, if you want me to."

Taylor didn't have a lot of hope that two weeks was enough time since it had taken him three months to find Darlene, but he gave her his blessing. If anyone could track down a replacement, it would be Darlene. She had the instincts of a bloodhound.

He'd turned her loose a couple of times to track down information that might otherwise have required a private eye. She'd had it so fast, he'd been awed.

"You find me a couple of good candidates," he told her, trying to muster a smile. "I'll do the final interview."

"You bet. Just leave it to me. By the way, Caitlin's school called. The headmistress wants to talk to you."

"Did she say what it's about?" he asked. Given the way the day was going, his seven-year-old had probably burned the place down.

"Nope. Just that it was important. The number's right here." She handed him the message slip on the top of the pile. "Want me to place the call?"

Taylor shook his head. "I can do it."

A few minutes later he had Josephine Lawrence Patterson on the line. Every time he talked to her, he couldn't help imagining her whacking his knuckles with a ruler.

"Mr. Matthews, I'm worried about Caitlin," she announced in that direct fashion he'd always admired until now. Now it set off alarm bells.

"Is she sick?"

"Homesick is more like it. Perhaps you could pick her up this weekend for a visit?"

If there was a hint of censure in Ms. Patterson's tone, Taylor couldn't identify it. Still, he was filled with guilt. He'd had to go to Charleston the previous weekend and had canceled Caitlin's regular visit home. He hadn't allowed himself to hear any disappointment in her voice. In fact, he'd convinced himself she'd sounded happy about staying with her friends. Apparently, though, his daughter was almost as adept as he was at hiding her real feelings. It wasn't a trait he was particularly proud about handing down.

"Please tell her I'll pick her up on Friday afternoon."

"Isn't that something you should tell her yourself?" she said, and this time the mild rebuke was clear.

"Of course. I'll call later today, when classes are out. Thank you, Ms. Patterson. It means a lot to me to know how well you look out for Caitlin."

"She's a lovely child, Mr. Matthews. I wish...well, I wish your circumstances were different."

"So do I, Ms. Patterson," he said. "So do I."

For some reason, as he spoke, an image of Zelda immediately came to mind. He did his damnedest to banish it before it could land him in a heap of misery.

Less than a week later, just when Taylor had almost managed to block Darlene's imminent departure from his mind, she showed up with the astonishing news that she'd found the ideal person to be her replacement, someone with seven years of legal secretary experience, plus paralegal training.

"In Port William?" Taylor said, regarding her skeptically.

"Yeah. Isn't that great? She just moved here. Perfect timing, huh? It's like an omen or something."

Omen was not the word that popped into Taylor's mind. A slow, steady pounding throbbed in his head as he guessed exactly who Darlene had discovered. Unless someone had had visitors he'd heard nothing about, only one person had returned to Port William in recent weeks. He'd been clinging desperately to the idea that her return was not permanent enough to require employment. Apparently the gods were dead set on making his life hell.

"Darlene, tell me you are not talking about Zelda Lane."

If she heard the panicked note in his voice, she didn't let on. "Why, of course, I am," she said blithely. "I'd forgotten you know her because of the will and all. She'll be terrific, don't you think?"

The only thing terrific Taylor could think of was the fact that Darlene was too young to recall his prior relationship with Zelda. At least she'd created this awkward situation innocently. Perhaps it wasn't too late to steer her toward looking for some other candidate for the job.

"You haven't said anything to her, have you?" he inquired, though admittedly without much hope. Darlene was not known for her reticence.

"You mean about the job? Sure. I told her all about it, about what a great boss you are."

"Did you happen to mention my name?"

Darlene regarded him blankly. "I didn't need to. You're the only lawyer in town. Everyone knows that."

"But she might not, especially if she just moved here." It was his only hope, that Zelda would back out of the interview the minute she found out who she'd be working for. The prospect of having her here, in this office, not more than two dozen steps from his bedroom, made his pulse kick.

"Oh, she knows," Darlene announced blithely. "In fact, she's sitting out front right now, waiting for the interview I scheduled." She studied him worriedly. "Boss, you look kinda funny. Did I do something wrong? I mean, I could tell her you're busy or something."

Wrong, he thought, trying not to panic at the understatement. Bringing Zelda into this office wasn't wrong. It was flat-out guaranteed emotional suicide.

Zelda wasn't sure what had possessed her to agree to an interview with Taylor. Not that Darlene hadn't been persuasive. That girl could sell pinecones to someone living in the forest. She'd swooped down on Zelda with so much enthusiasm that Zelda had almost forgotten exactly who it was Darlene wanted her to work for. To her astonishment, she'd found herself nodding and agreeing to show up this morning, even though she hadn't even decided whether or not to stay in Port William. She'd even used Harlan's brand new machine to fax Kate for a letter of recommendation. She'd told herself she was just going through the motions, that it was a way to get under Taylor's skin. She couldn't think of anyone more deserving of a little discomfort.

Now here she was in Taylor's reception area, wearing one of her best business suits in a turquoise fabric that matched her eyes, and wondering if she'd gone and lost her mind. What had gotten into her?

Perhaps it was that same quirky streak that always encouraged her to do the unexpected. Perhaps it was a desire to see the look on Taylor's face when she walked into his office. Perhaps, if she was prepared to admit the truth, it was a deep-seated desire to show him and everyone else in this town that she was an intelligent, responsible woman and not the flake they all remembered.

Not that she needed to prove anything to anyone at this late date, she told herself staunchly. She knew who she was. Wasn't that all that really mattered?

She was just about satisfied with that mature, rational explanation, when Darlene announced that Taylor was ready to see her. Her heart thumped unsteadily as she walked into his sedate, mahogany-paneled office, an office she could have described down to the last detail in advance thanks to all the times he'd daydreamed aloud to her about how it would look one day. The genuine surge of pleasure she felt at the expression of absolute bewilderment on Taylor's face told her that all that stuff about maturity was so much hogwash. She liked seeing Taylor shaken up. Even more, she supposed, she liked knowing she could be the one to do it.

As soon as the door closed behind Darlene, Taylor started shaking his head.

"Zelda, I can't imagine what you're doing here. You know this isn't a good idea."

Thoroughly enjoying herself now that she'd admitted to herself why she'd come, she regarded him innocently. "Why is that?" she inquired sweetly.

"It just isn't. There's too much..." His voice trailed off.

"Chemistry?" she suggested, to fill the conversational void.

Taylor glared at her. "No, damn it."

"History?"

He rubbed his temples. "Zelda, it's just a bad idea. I can't make it any plainer than that."

"You don't think I'm qualified?" she asked. She pushed the recommendation from Kate across the desk. "I think my letter of reference speaks for itself."

He glanced at the letterhead, obviously prepared to dismiss it. She could tell the precise instant when the name registered. Thanks to some highly publicized celebrity cases, Kate Newton had a national reputation as a crackerjack divorce lawyer. His eyes widened as he read every glowing word Kate had written. He cleared his throat.

"Well, your former boss certainly speaks quite highly of your work," he admitted.

Zelda tried not to gloat. "Yes," she said briskly. "Now, then, if we're agreed that I'm more than qualified for the job, what exactly is the problem?"

Taylor was too much the lawyer to say anything that might later be used against him in a discrimination suit. Zelda regarded him smugly while he struggled to find a suitable answer that wouldn't fuel her desire for revenge for his walking out on her. He choked back every response that apparently came to mind, then finally settled for saying, "I thought you were going back to Los Angeles."

She had to admit she enjoyed the little hint of desperation in his voice. "I never said that," she corrected.

"Then you've decided to fulfill the terms of the will?"

"Let's just say that knowing I'd have a job would make me more inclined to stick around. So, what's it going to be, Taylor? Do I have the job or not?"

He regarded her intently. "Zelda, are you sure you want to do this?"

"You mean, stay in Port William?"

"No. I mean, do you seriously want to work for me?"

It was the closest he'd come to conceding that she might have cause not to want to be in the same room with him. She leveled a perfectly bland look straight at him. "It's a job, Taylor. It happens to be one I'm trained for. Beyond that, I don't think there are any other considerations."

Her defiant gaze dared him to contradict her. Finally he sighed.

"I suppose we could give it a try."

Zelda nodded. "Shall we say, one month?"

"One month would be fine." He seemed to stumble over the response.

Zelda caught the distress he tried valiantly to hide and grinned. "I'll see you bright and early Monday morning, then. I can't tell you how much I'm looking forward to it."

Taylor looked as if he'd rather eat dirt.

## Chapter Four

Unfortunately, Zelda didn't realize until she was walking back home that her perverse desire to rattle Taylor had overcome her own instincts for self-preservation. If she'd managed to open Taylor's eyes to another side of her personality thanks to Kate's glowing recommendation, then he had taught her something, as well. All Taylor Matthews had to do to make her pulse flutter was breathe. That was it. His mere existence in a room set her heart racing.

There was no reasoning with a reaction like that. Without half trying, Taylor made her want to do all those wicked, outrageous things that had so appalled the straitlaced people of Port William a decade ago, the very things that had sent Taylor himself scurrying out of her life.

And she had just agreed to go to work for the man! She'd probably be chasing *him* around his desk by the end of the first week.

Since such clear evidence that her daredevil streak was far from dead appalled her, she stopped by Sarah Lynn's for something calorie-laden to combat outright depression. A hot-fudge sundae ought to do it. The more decadent, the better.

Though it was early for the lunch crowd, at least half a dozen people were lingering over coffee and gossip. Since all conversation stopped the minute she walked in, Zelda had a hunch she was the current topic. It was hardly the first time, but it made her uncomfortable just the same. She suddenly longed for L.A., where the only people who knew her name were the ones she told.

Though most of the faces at the counter were familiar, she merely waved a greeting. She pointedly avoided making the sort of eye contact that would invite anyone to join her. As she headed for the nearest empty booth, Sarah Lynn bustled out from the kitchen and embraced her. She smelled of cinnamon and apples. It must be apple crisp day, served hot and topped by melting vanilla ice cream, Zelda recalled as she returned Sarah Lynn's hug.

That hug and the genuine warmth behind it brought the salty sting of tears to Zelda's eyes for the first time since she'd gotten home. Just being in this place, with the scent of fresh-baked pies in the air and the Formica and chrome polished to a spotless gleam, was enough to carry her back in time. She had more happy memories here than she did of that house a few blocks away.

"Zelda, honey, I've been wondering just when you were going to come to see me," Sarah Lynn said in a tone that gently scolded her for the delay. "Now sit right down here and tell me all about Hollywood. Have you met any stars out there? Why, I'll bet you know Kevin Costner."

She sighed dreamily at the prospect, a reaction that seemed somewhat unexpected from a woman edging toward sixty and built as solidly as one of those mowers over at Harlan's. Zelda knew, though, that Sarah Lynn's practical, down-to-earth nature hid a romantic streak almost as wide as her own mama's had been.

Laughing at the evidence of it, Zelda shook her head. "Sorry to disappoint you, but I've never met him. I did arrive at a restaurant one night right after he'd left with carry-out. Does that count?"

"Not for much," Sarah Lynn said with a laugh. "Well, never you mind. What can I get you, hon?"

"A hot-fudge sundae," Zelda said at once. "The biggest one you can make."

Sarah Lynn didn't remind her that it was before noon. She'd never been one to criticize her customers' dietary whims. Given her cholesterol-laden menu, it would have been decidedly bad for business. "Extra whipped cream, the way you always liked it?" she said immediately.

The one thing Zelda had always known about small-town living was that people never forgot anything—good or bad. In this case, it genuinely made her feel as if she'd come home. "Of course."

When Sarah Lynn brought the sundae with its mound of freshly whipped cream and sprinkle of nuts, she settled down opposite Zelda. Her expression turned sober.

"I don't have much time before this place gets busier than rush hour at a train station, but tell me how you're doing. I want the truth, too, not one of those polite evasions you use with acquaintances. You getting along okay out at the house? I know you must miss your mama."

Zelda paused with a spoonful of ice cream halfway to her mouth and said softly, "Yes, I do. I don't think I really accepted that she was gone until I came back here."

"They buried her next to your daddy, just like you asked. I planted some mums. I thought she'd like that. You been out to the cemetery?"

Zelda shook her head. "I couldn't. Not yet."

"Well, never mind. You'll go when you're ready."

"Did people talk because I didn't make it back for the funeral?"

"Honey, people in this town always talk. Ain't no point in worrying about it. Besides, we all handle things the best way we can."

Zelda sighed, grateful that this woman to whom she'd once been so close wasn't making any judgments. She regarded Sarah Lynn with genuine fondness. "You were one of the few people in this town who really understood what she was like, you know. You never judged her. Or me. I always appreciated that."

"Maybe because I knew what it was like to have dreams go awry." She reached over and patted Zelda's hand. "Whatever her idiosyncrasies, she loved you, honey. I know that as surely as I know the sun comes up in the morning."

Zelda had known that, too, but it didn't hurt to be reminded, especially now when her mother's final act seemed to contradict the fact. Maybe Sarah Lynn was the one who could explain Ella Louise's whim.

"Do you know why she wanted me to come back here and stay, then?" she asked, unable to keep a trace of bitterness out of her voice. "How could she insist on that when she knew how much I hated it, when she knew I had a new life in Los Angeles?"

Sarah Lynn didn't show the slightest hint of surprise at Zelda's question. Obviously news of the will's terms had reached her. Either that or Ella Louise had discussed them with her. Apparently not the latter, Zelda realized with regret as Sarah Lynn shook her head.

"She never said a thing about her will or about wanting you back here, at least not straight out. She did worry about you being all the way out in California, though. We talked about it more than once."

The response only added to Zelda's confusion. "She never gave me a clue that she was worried. She never was the kind of mother to issue warnings about every little thing. Besides, it's no more dangerous in L.A. than anyplace else these days."

"Hon, I don't think it was crime that worried her."

Before Zelda could ask her what she meant by her cryptic remark, the diner's door opened and a half dozen customers flocked in. Sarah Lynn patted her hand once again. "Let's get together real soon. You need anything in the meantime, you just give me a holler."

Since there seemed to be no point in trying to pursue the conversation now when Sarah Lynn was distracted, Zelda just squeezed her hand. "Thanks. It's good to see you."

Sarah Lynn winked at her. "And don't you let Taylor work you too hard."

Zelda stared after her in astonishment. It seemed some things in Port William never changed. She and Taylor were still making news.

That afternoon Zelda put on a pair of shorts and an old shirt she'd found hanging on the back of a hook in the bathroom. She knotted the shirttails at her waist, then settled down on the front porch with a glass of iced tea. The sun filtered through the trees in a way that made the yard seem prettier than it was. She barely noticed it. She figured it was time she had a serious talk with herself.

It appeared she'd decided to stay in Port William, despite whatever misgivings she might have had only a few short hours ago. Her conversation with Sarah Lynn had only confirmed that her mother had wanted her back here for some very specific reason. She had to stay long enough to figure out what that was, or at least to satisfy herself that it had been no more than a flighty whim.

The decision to stay made, that left her to wrestle with the equally troubling matter of Taylor Matthews. She reminded herself that nothing was likely to start up with Taylor again unless she allowed it. She told herself that pride alone ought to keep her from forgiving him too quickly for the way he'd treated her. And then she conceded dryly that Taylor hadn't exactly looked as if he was interested in spending eight hours a day in an office with her, much less pursuing anything more personal.

The last thought fueled enough anger that she left the porch and grabbed up all the old hooked rugs in the house and took them out to the clothesline in back. Then she proceeded to beat the daylights out of them. Clouds of dust swirled around her and left her sneezing. She backed up in search of fresh air and bumped straight into something solid. She knew from the way the goose bumps instantaneously rose all over her that the something was Taylor. His low chuckle confirmed it and sent sparks scampering straight down her spine.

"Taking out your frustrations on the carpet?" he inquired in a lazy drawl that was friendlier than just about anything else he'd said to her since her return.

"Just cleaning," she said. She kept her tone curt so he wouldn't guess how that drawl of his affected her. "What are you doing here?"

"I've been thinking about something ever since you left my office this morning."

"Oh?" She glanced up and looked into troubled gray eyes that immediately cut away from hers. "What would that be?"

He started to say something, then stopped. Finally, after some internal struggle she couldn't begin to fathom, he said, "We never discussed salary. I can't afford to pay what you were making in Los Angeles."

Zelda could tell from his uneasy expression that her pay was not what had brought him out here. "You trying to wriggle out of our deal?"

"No, but this arrangement's going to be difficult enough without any misunderstandings. I just wanted to be up-front with you about a potential problem."

"That would be a pleasant change." The sarcasm crept out before she could stop it.

Looking guilty, he shoved his hands in his pockets. "Damn it, Zelda, you're not making this any easier."

She regarded him evenly. "Is there some reason why I should?"

He groaned. "Okay, I can see you're still angry. I suppose you have every right to be."

"Suppose?" she echoed incredulously. Ten years' worth of rage exploded. Caution flew out the window. She poked a finger in his chest. His rock-solid chest. She tried not to let that distract her from her fury.

"You suppose? Taylor Matthews, I was in love with you," she blurted out to her regret. Once she'd said that, there didn't seem to be much point in holding back. "You led me to believe you felt the same way. Then the minute your daddy suggested I might be a liability to the long-range political ambitions of the Matthews family, you dumped me with no more concern than you would have felt swatting a fly. I'd say that gives me cause to be angry."

He leveled a gaze at her that almost took her breath away. It seemed he was looking straight into her soul. "It's been a long time now," he reminded her.

His apparent conviction that time should have healed her wounds just riled her up all over again.

"Being told you're not good enough isn't all that easy to forget," she informed him. "I thought you were the one person in town I could count on, the one person who didn't give a damn about my mama's eccentricities, the one person who cared about *me,* no matter what. Instead, you bailed out on me when my reputation got a little inconvenient, a reputation, I might add, that you had contributed considerably to creating.''

''It wasn't your reputation... I mean, not exactly,'' he began unconvincingly, then held up his hands. ''Never mind. I can see coming by here was a bad idea. I'll see you on Monday.''

Watching Taylor turn around and start to walk away in the middle of a fight infuriated Zelda almost more than any words he could have spoken. He hadn't taken half a dozen steps when she instinctively flew after him, leaping on him from behind. Her arms looped around his neck and her knees dug into his sides as if she'd jumped astride a runaway horse.

''What the hell...?'' he muttered just as they fell to the ground in a tangle. The air whooshed out of him as he landed with an ungraceful thud. Zelda's own fall was cushioned, but she was beyond caring if she broke every bone in both their bodies.

''Damn you, Taylor Matthews, don't you dare walk away from me like that again,'' she shouted, pummeling his back with her fists.

He was absolutely still beneath the onslaught. In fact, he took it for a full minute, allowing her to vent her fury. Then, before she could catch her breath, he flipped her over as if she were no more trouble than a gnat and pinned her to the ground. She felt an almost forgotten surge of excitement race through her as she saw the angry sparks in his eyes. This was the man she'd adored, the man filled with passion, the man who tilted at windmills, the man who'd lavished more tenderness on her than both her parents combined.

"Come on, Taylor, fight with me," she taunted. "Used to be we argued half the night away, then spent the rest of it making up."

She could feel the heat rising in his body, even as his stormy expression gave way to something far more dangerous. Suddenly, just as she realized exactly what she'd set loose, his fingers were cupping her head and his mouth was on hers—hot, urgent, demanding. Years of pent-up hunger were in the kiss that shocked then thrilled with its deepening intensity. There was no tenderness on his part, no hint of gentle longing, just a raw, primitive need. Deep inside Zelda, a matching need exploded, even as it set off warning bells that clanged so loudly only an idiot would have ignored them.

"Taylor," she murmured, too softly, too ineffectively. Her body, crushed beneath his, seemed to have a will of its own. Even as her mind screamed that she needed to get away, her hips arched to fit more intimately with his, seeking the source of the heat that had raged between them as quickly as a brushfire.

It had always been this way with them. Always.

*And it never solved anything,* a voice inside her warned.

This time Zelda listened. She shoved hard against Taylor's chest, tumbling him off her. He looked at her and groaned, his expression torn between guilt and a desire he couldn't do a thing to hide.

"I will not allow this to happen," he muttered under his breath, as if a sheer act of will was all that was required to shatter an unbreakable bond.

She glared at him. "What, Taylor? What is it you won't allow?"

"This," he said, waving his hand to encompass the two of them, the ground, their rumpled clothes.

"You were the one who kissed me," she reminded him.

"I'm not denying that," he snapped, scrambling back to his feet and brushing the grass off his suit. "It was a foolish mistake, okay? It won't happen again."

Zelda watched him flee, then murmured with an odd sense of exhilaration, "Bet it will."


"Taylor, what's this I hear about Zelda Lane being back?" Beau Matthews asked that night over dinner.

Taylor almost choked on a mouthful of black-eyed peas. Given the events of that very afternoon, he viewed Zelda as an even more dangerous topic than usual. He glanced toward his mother, appealing to her to switch the direction of the conversation. Unfortunately she didn't take the hint.

"I saw her myself," Geraldine Matthews said. "She was sitting in the diner before lunchtime, talking to Sarah Lynn. She looked even lovelier than I recalled.''

"There is nothing lovely about that girl," Beau said. "She's trouble. Always has been. That mother of hers was a drunk. If you ask me, Zelda's bound to turn out just like her."

The comment made Taylor see red. "Dad, you don't know a thing in the world about what Zelda's been doing the past ten years," he retorted, defending her now as he should have done long ago. Guilt for his past silence gnawed at him, even as he tried belatedly to make his father see reason. "People change. She's had a responsible job with a very important lawyer out in California."

Beau's head snapped up. "Now how would you know a thing like that, unless you'd seen her? You haven't seen her, have you?"

"As a matter of fact, I asked Taylor to see to Ella Louise's will," his mother chimed in, shooting a warning glance at him. "Naturally, he's had to see Zelda."

"Now why would you go and do a damn fool thing like that?" Beau demanded, his anger now directed at the pair of them. "You know the last thing Taylor needs is to get mixed up with that girl again."

Taylor stood up slowly and glowered at his father. "Dad, I'm past the age where you can control who I do or don't see. Maybe if I hadn't been such a damned idiot ten years ago and hadn't listened to you, my life would have turned out differently."

Ignoring his father's stunned expression, he leaned down and kissed his mother's cheek. "Thank you for dinner. I think I'd best be going before Dad and I wind up saying things we're likely to regret."

"I don't believe in regrets, son," his father shouted after him.

"I know," Taylor said softly. "More's the pity."

As he drove back toward town, he was thankful he'd managed to keep quiet about hiring Zelda to work in his office. Of course it was only a matter of time before the news reached Beau. Well, that was just something he'd have to deal with when the time came. He'd had his reasons for hiring her . . . though damned if he could think of a one of them at the moment.

He sighed heavily. How different things might have been if he'd listened to his heart all those years ago instead of paying attention to his father's misguided if well-intentioned demands!

He'd played things by the book, though. He'd finished law school, married a girl from the best sorority on campus, one with all the right bloodlines—a descendant of the original South Carolina settlers, no less. They'd bought a fancy house in Charleston. He'd joined the most prestigious law firm in town, thanks to Maribeth's family influence. Caitlin had been born almost nine months to the day after the wedding, right on time, with a minimum of fuss.

Within a year Taylor had been positioned to run for public office. Beau had been ecstatic. His golden boy was exactly where he wanted him, on schedule and destined for greatness.

At the time it hadn't seemed to matter much to Taylor that he was miserable. There was little time for introspection, anyway. Maybe if he'd stopped long enough to take a good long look at his life and his marriage, things wouldn't have turned out the way they had.

Without realizing what he was doing, he found himself instinctively driving by Zelda's house. Those five minutes this afternoon when he'd disregarded every warning and kissed the woman senseless had been the first time he'd felt alive in more years than he could recall.

But it wouldn't work between them, not after all the lessons he'd learned. Zelda was high-spirited and impetuous, a combination that had very nearly destroyed him once. He wouldn't risk that kind of anguish again.

## Chapter Five

Zelda marched into Taylor's office on Monday morning with her shoulders squared and her head held high. She was determined that Taylor would never detect even the tiniest hint of the nervousness she felt. She wore another power suit just to make a statement—black this time. There was nothing more professional than basic black.

Admittedly, though, her uneasiness had nothing to do with the job. She knew after working for Kate that she could handle the workload of a small-town lawyer with one hand tied behind her. It was the memory of that unexpected, searing kiss that had her jumpy as a June bug.

Fortunately the first person she saw when she walked into Taylor's office was Darlene, not her new boss.

"Hey, there," Darlene said, beaming. "You're right on time. Today should be a light day. Mr. Matthews had to take Caitlin back to school. Then he planned to go on over to Charleston to file some motions in a case he's handling over there."

Zelda stopped in her tracks. "Caitlin?" she questioned, her pulse hammering.

"His daughter," Darlene said, totally unaware that she'd just dropped a bombshell of atomic proportions. "Haven't you met her yet? She's the cutest little thing. She'll be eight pretty soon. Looks just like her daddy. She's in boarding school, has been ever since..." She paused and bit her lip. "Well, maybe that's something you ought to hear about from Mr. Matthews. He wouldn't want me gossiping about his personal life."

Of all the times for Darlene to decide to hold her tongue, Zelda thought in frustration. She didn't dare probe too deeply for fear the talkative Darlene would later mention her interest to Taylor.

"All lawyers rely on their secretaries' discretion," she said diplomatically. "I'm sure he must appreciate yours. Of course, if I'm going to be working here, it would help to know if I should expect his wife and daughter to be popping in, and whether he minds being disturbed."

To Zelda's regret, Darlene grinned mischievously. Obviously she was quicker than Zelda had given her credit for being.

"Oh, Mr. Matthews will fill you in on all that kind of thing, I'm sure," she said. She regarded Zelda speculatively. "You know I was talking to my mother about you. She remembers you from when you lived here before."

"Oh, really?"

"Her name's Jeannie Wilson. She'd already had my older sister, that's Danielle, by then. Anyway, she said you and Taylor—I mean, Mr. Matthews—well, that you had something real special going."

"We were friends," Zelda said a little too emphatically.

Darlene regarded her disbelievingly. "Sounded to me like it was a whole lot more than that."

"Well, you know how rumors are."

"How come you didn't mention any of that when I asked you if you wanted to apply for my job? I mean, I knew you knew him because of his doing your mama's will and all, but I'd never guessed about the rest."

"It hardly seemed relevant," Zelda said.

"Yeah, I suppose not. My mother said you split up and then you left for California."

"That's about it," Zelda agreed, knowing that the capsulized version didn't begin to cover all the heartache involved. "Darlene, don't you think we ought to get to work?"

Darlene blinked at the pointed suggestion. "Oh, yeah, sure. I guess we should. Mr. Matthews told me to explain which cases he's working on, where we keep things, that sort of stuff. Mondays are usually pretty busy because he sits in that house all weekend long with his dictating machine. I spend the whole day typing."

"Perhaps I should do that today," Zelda suggested. "I ought to get used to it while you're still around to explain how he likes his letters and notes done."

"Why, sure," Darlene replied, looking pleased at being considered an expert on her boss's ways. Suddenly her complexion turned chalk-white. "Whoops! 'Scuse me," she exclaimed, and raced for the bathroom.

While Darlene dealt with her morning sickness, Zelda moved into position behind the computer terminal. Judging from the instruction books piled up, the office clearly had the most up-to-date programs. As soon as Darlene returned, she pointed out the codes, all of which were exactly like the standard ones Zelda was used to.

"I think I'm all set," she said finally.

"Then I'll just try to catch up on some of this filing," Darlene said. "Mr. Matthews pulls files and leaves 'em scattered all around when he's done, especially on weekends. Then he yells like crazy because he can't find what he's looking for."

Sounded just like Taylor, Zelda thought wryly. When push came to shove, he apparently never could take the blame for his mistakes. She certainly knew that firsthand.

By midafternoon she had caught up on the typing and she and Darlene had finished the filing. The filing had taken longer than usual because Darlene kept throwing up. Worried by the expectant mother's pallor, Zelda sent her home.

Left alone, she sat quietly for a minute trying to absorb the fact that she was actually working in Taylor's office. Her gaze was drawn toward the wall that separated the work space from his home.

She hadn't heard a sound from next door all morning. Did that mean there was no wife, after all? Was that what Darlene had refrained from telling her, that Taylor and his wife were divorced? Or was it something more? She tried to imagine what might have made Taylor send a seven-year-old off to boarding school. Surely it wasn't just that he didn't like the role of single parent? He had always talked about how much he wanted kids, lots of them, since he'd been an only child.

When she tired of coming up with questions for which she could think of no answers, she picked up the morning's work and took it into Taylor's office. As she stacked the letters for his signature and the file notes for him to look over, she spotted the silver-framed photograph of a child in a swing. She glanced around, but could find no companion picture of the girl's mother. She couldn't resist picking up the photo of Caitlin to study it more closely, even though it was a poignant reminder that she had once hoped to share a family with Taylor.

With her fingers trembling more than they should, she touched the glass. The lovely, pint-size angel appeared to be about six or seven, which meant the picture had to be fairly recent. Her face was flushed, her black curls in disarray, but it was the devilish sparkle in her eyes that enchanted Zelda. How many times had she seen that exact same gleam in Taylor's eyes right before he'd led them both into some mischief?

"Oh, I'll bet you're a handful," she murmured, somehow pleased by the thought despite the pang of longing deep in her heart.

She had just replaced the photo on his desk when she sensed Taylor's presence. Thanks to the thick carpeting, she hadn't heard a sound. A guilty heat crept into her cheeks as she looked into eyes the exact color of storm clouds.

"Hi," she said, offering a tentative smile that wasn't returned. "I was just putting the work we did this morning on your desk."

His gaze went from the photo to her and back again, proving that he'd arrived before she'd put it down. The angles in his face looked harsher than ever. Whatever he was thinking, though, he kept to himself.

"Where's Darlene?" he asked finally.

"We were all caught up, so I suggested she go on home. She had a rough morning."

For the first time he actually looked directly at her in a way that wasn't condemning. "Rough how?" he asked.

She was pleased by the genuine concern in his voice. It proved he wasn't as heartless as he sometimes liked to pretend. "Morning sickness," she told him. "It's come on with a vengeance. I hope you don't mind that I let her go."

He shook his head and eased past her to sit behind the desk. "Of course not. Everything quiet around here?"

"Harlan wants to stop by when it's convenient to talk about filing suit against one of his suppliers. I scheduled him for ten tomorrow morning. He told me a little about the case, and I looked up some of the case law for you. The notes are on top of that stack to your left."

If he was startled or pleased by her initiative, he didn't display it by so much as the flicker of an eyelash. "Fine. Anything else?"

Oddly disgruntled by his failure to react, she shook her head. "I'll be at my desk if you need me."

At the door, she hesitated. "Taylor?"

He glanced up.

"How do I handle it if your wife calls or drops by when you're busy? Should I interrupt you?"

The haunted expression that washed over his face stunned her. "That's not something you'll have to worry about," he said, his curt tone so cold it could have chilled wine. "Now, if you'll excuse me, I have work to do."

The abrupt dismissal stung. Back in the outer office, Zelda wondered if these first few minutes were an indication of the way things were going to be from now on. Taylor hadn't done anything she could rightfully complain about. He had been thoroughly professional, even if somewhat distant, right up until she'd mentioned his wife.

What on earth had gone wrong in that marriage? Whatever it was, Taylor was still clearly distraught by it. Zelda felt her heart wrench as she thought of Caitlin. What effect would such obvious anguish have on that beautiful, lively little child of his?

It was none of her business, she reminded herself sharply. None. She was just passing through Taylor's life again.

As the door to his office closed, Taylor shoved his trembling fingers through his hair and muttered a curse. Why the hell had he taken his anger at Maribeth and events that had happened a lifetime ago out on Zelda? He'd seen the unmistakable flash of hurt in her eyes, the proud tilt of her chin. Damn it, she wasn't just being nosy. As a new secretary, she'd made a perfectly natural inquiry. She couldn't possibly know the story of his disastrous marriage and its tragic outcome. Beau Matthews had seen to it that the worst of it never reached the media. It was one of the rare times that Taylor had been grateful for his father's power and influence. What little gossip that had made the rounds was bad enough. Sooner or later he'd have to tell Zelda at least that much of it or someone else in town was bound to do it first. Heaven knew how they would embellish it, but he doubted he'd come out the hero.

In the meantime, though, he had to find some way to coexist with Zelda for the next month without letting her very presence rattle him. Walking in here today, seeing her at his desk, had brought on a flood of old daydreams.

Once they'd talked for hours on end about how much he wanted to have an office that was attached to his home, so his family—Zelda and all of their adorable, redheaded little children—would be close by.

Well, that hadn't happened, he reminded himself fiercely. He hadn't married Zelda. His wife, well, he didn't even want to think about Maribeth. And his beautiful, precious daughter was away at boarding school so he wouldn't have to cope with raw memories that hurt too much. It shouldn't have been this way, but nobody ever said life came with guarantees.

Suddenly he recalled the very first time he'd been truly aware that the redheaded daredevil who was two classes behind him in school was something more than a pint-size pest. He'd thought of her as little else than a girl who was always anxious to follow his lead, who always looked at him with the kind of adoration he hadn't deserved, but which had made him feel ten feet tall. He'd been a rebellious kid. Zelda had been a more than willing co-conspirator.

He'd been a sophomore in high school when that had changed. Zelda had still been in junior high. In age difference it hadn't been much. In terms of pretended sophistication, it had been light-years.

Even so, like a bolt from the blue, he'd noticed the endlessly long legs, the already curvaceous figure, the hair that gleamed like fire in the sun. His pal, his best friend, had grown up on him.

Unfortunately, he wasn't the only one aware of the changes. When he'd first recognized that he was thinking of her differently, Zelda had been cornered outside Sarah Lynn's by a half dozen taunting boys, whose tasteless comments were fueled more by rampaging hormones than cruelty.

Driven by some primitive instinct, Taylor had been about to rush to her rescue when he'd noticed the sparks in her eyes and recognized that the fourteen-year-old wasn't intimidated. She was furious. He knew better than to get on the wrong side of Zelda's temper, but her assailants obviously didn't. Bobby Daniels had missed the signs completely and made one taunting comment too many. Zelda's knee had caught him strategically and a left hook bloodied his nose. The stunned, open-mouthed boys had scattered, taking the moaning Bobby with them. Even Taylor had been awed.

"You throw a mean punch," Taylor recalled telling her, falling a little bit in love with her at that moment. He'd known then that she was destined to be a woman who'd be a spirited match for any man. As young as he'd been, he'd wanted desperately to be that man. "How'd you learn to fight?"

"Practice," she'd retorted with an expression he couldn't fathom.

Then she'd sashayed into Sarah Lynn's and ordered a hamburger, fries and a hot-fudge sundae as if punching out a bully had only whetted her appetite. She hadn't even blinked when an irate Patty Sue Daniels had stormed in a few minutes later to threaten Zelda with jail for decking her precious son.

"Go ahead," she'd said, calm as you please. "But you won't like hearing the filth that was coming out of his mouth testified to in court."

"Who'd believe you?" Patty Sue had retorted derisively. "Everybody in town knows your mama's a mental case and that you're just like her."

Zelda had turned pale at that, every drop of color washing out of her skin. Her hands had clenched into fists once more. She'd slid off her stool at the counter, her intentions clear to anyone who knew her as well as Taylor did. Before she could deck Patty Sue, Taylor had interceded, even though he figured the obnoxious woman deserved whatever she got.

"I heard him, too," he'd said, stepping between them. "Think the judge and jury will believe me? Let me see now, what were his exact words?" In a low voice he'd repeated Bobby's remarks word for word, avoiding Zelda's gaze the whole time.

Patty Sue had turned red as a beet while listening to the crude remarks. "I ought to tan your hide, young man. Or maybe I ought to have a word with your daddy. Nobody talks that way to a lady."

"Exactly," he'd said. "But I'm not the one you ought to be explaining that to."

Patty Sue had left in a huff. Considering how gingerly Bobby had inched into his seat in class the next morning, apparently his mother had taken Taylor's advice to heart. Even after all these years, the memory made him chuckle. He doubted if the town's newly elected mayor—*Robert* Daniels—would recall the incident so fondly.

That defiant spark in Zelda that had first fascinated him had been very much in evidence on Friday when he'd made the foolish mistake of stopping by her house. She was still a hellion, all right. And she could still pack a wallop. He had the bruises on his back to prove it.

And, no matter how much he might hate it, he was still fascinated. This time, though, he'd die before he'd do a damned thing about it. He sighed and wondered exactly how many times he'd need to remind himself of that over the coming weeks.

After that first awkward day, Zelda told herself things had to improve. Instead, each day turned into torment. They were both so polite it made her want to scream. She wasn't sure what she'd expected, but it wasn't this cool civility. Taylor was a good lawyer, smart and instinctive, and more than willing to listen to her suggestions. He was even lavish with his praise, though most often it came in the form of notes jotted on the corner of papers she'd written for him. The ideal boss.

Unfortunately, Zelda had wanted her old friend back, if not her old lover.

She made it through the first week and then the second. By the third she was ready to admit that this had been the third worst mistake of her life. The first had been falling in love with Taylor all those years ago. The second had been not getting over him.

She ought to quit. She sat at the computer, glaring at his office, and tried to convince herself to walk out and go back to Los Angeles where life was far less complicated.

"You are not a quitter," she snapped finally. "You are not."

Suddenly she realized she was not alone. She looked up from her computer and caught Taylor watching her with something akin to longing on his face. It was the first tangible sign she'd had that he didn't outright loathe her for putting them both into this awkward situation.

"Is everything okay?" she asked, her voice far too breathless to suit her. Obviously she was reading too much into that unguarded expression she'd just witnessed, an expression that had vanished faster than a wisp of smoke.

"I suppose I was just wondering why I never realized you were so..." He fumbled for a word.

"Smart? Responsible?" Zelda supplied with an automatic edge of sarcasm. Then her innate good humor crept in. Her tone lighter, she taunted, "It's hard to pick up on things like that when you're skinny-dipping at one in the morning or sneaking into Sarah Lynn's to make ice-cream sundaes in the dark."

Taylor's gaze softened. His chuckle crept in and, like a touch of spring air, it warmed her heart.

"It's a good thing Sarah Lynn has a forgiving nature, or we'd have served time for that one," he said.

"It was still the best hot-fudge sundae I ever had," she replied, unable to keep the wistful note from her voice.

A smile tilted the corners of his mouth, then disappeared in a beat. "Yeah, me, too."

While Zelda stared after him with her heart thudding, he quietly closed the door to his office. Now what, she wondered, was that all about?

## Chapter Six

That fleeting moment under Taylor's speculative gaze was the last straw. He'd looked so lost, so lonely in that one instant when his expression hadn't been guarded. Why? What had happened to him over the past ten years to rob him of the zest for living they had once shared?

Darlene had already whetted Zelda's curiosity about what had gone on in Taylor's life while she'd been in Los Angeles. No one so far had satisfied that curiosity, and she had never tolerated secrets very well. Maybe that's why she'd taken the paralegal courses, so she could be in a profession that allowed her to probe behind the facade most people displayed to the public and get at the truth of their lives.

Her one attempt to get Taylor to say anything about his marriage had failed miserably. Obviously if she was going to learn a thing, someone else would have to be the one to tell her. She sorted through the possibilities and picked Elsie Whittingham.

Elsie was lonely. She liked to talk. She had once provided an after-school refuge for Zelda. And she knew more about what went on in Port William than any other ten people combined, with the possible exception of Sarah Lynn. Zelda didn't dare ask her old friend. Sarah Lynn might care about Zelda as if she were her own daughter, but she was also loyal to Taylor. Zelda didn't want to test that loyalty.

That night on her way home from work, she stopped by Elsie's for a glass of lemonade and some of her homemade gingersnaps. It wasn't the first time she'd dropped in unannounced, acting on an old habit from childhood. But this evening was the first time she'd shown any interest in lingering beyond a few polite minutes. Elsie beamed as Zelda settled in a chair in front of the fireplace and sipped on her second glass of lemonade.

"First fire of the season," Elsie said. "There's a real bite in the air tonight."

"Feels good," Zelda said, referring as much to the chill outside as to the blazing warmth of the fire. She was enjoying the real changing of the seasons again.

"I sure am glad to have you stop by now and again," Elsie added. "You remember how you used to do this when you were a girl? I recall it like it was yesterday. You always did love my gingersnaps. You and Taylor both. I must have baked twice a week just to keep you two satisfied.''

''That was Taylor. He could eat a dozen for every two I got.'' She sighed. ''Mama never baked,'' she added wistfully. ''Never cooked if she could help it. I used to pray that just once I'd come home from school and be able to sniff the scent of warm cookies fresh from the oven. Instead, all I ever smelled was bourbon.''

As soon as the words were out, Zelda regretted them. Keeping silent about her mother's drinking had once been habit. ''Sorry. I shouldn't have said that.''

''And why not, I'd like to know?'' Elsie said indignantly. ''It wasn't right.''

Zelda suddenly felt the need to defend her mother…again. ''Mama did the best she could,'' she said sharply, trying to make up for her indiscreet remark just moments before. ''There were times when she was just fine, when she'd tell me stories or read to me from those books of hers. Sometimes she'd take down her big old atlas and point to places far away and talk about what it would be like to travel there. I knew more about geography by the time I was in grade school than some kids do when they graduate from college.''

Elsie pursed her lips. ''It was your father I always felt sorry for. Poor Joseph had no wife looking after his needs the way she should.''

Zelda felt as if an old wound had been stripped open. "That's not true," she said in a low voice. "It was his fault. You don't know what he was like."

"He was a fine, Christian man," Elsie insisted, looking shocked that Zelda would dare to suggest otherwise.

"He was selfish, rigid and judgmental. Why the hell do you think my mother drank in the first place?" she said furiously. "Because nothing she ever did was good enough to satisfy him. Not one blessed thing."

Stunned by her outburst, Zelda snapped her mouth shut before she revealed far more than she'd ever intended to say about the horror of living in that house with Joseph Lane. He punished not with spankings, not even with yelling, but with his cold silence. Just the memory of it made her freeze up inside.

She set her unfinished glass of lemonade down carefully. "I think I'd best be going."

Elsie regarded her worriedly. "There's no need for you to run off. Let's talk about something more pleasant. You shouldn't go getting yourself all upset over things that can't be changed. I'm sorry we got into it. All that was a long time ago. Tell me how things are going now that you're back. Are you settling in okay over there? Is there anything you need?"

Zelda drew in a deep breath and finally sat back. "I'm fine," she said. "Sooner or later I'm going to need to do something about the sorry state of the house, but for now I'm making do.''

Zelda saw the speculative look in Elsie's eyes. She could guess what was really on the woman's mind and since it would head the conversation in the direction she wanted, she just waited for curiosity to get the better of Elsie.

''You and Taylor getting along okay?'' she asked eventually.

''He's a good boss,'' Zelda said.

Elsie rolled her eyes at the bland remark. ''I wasn't referring to his dictating skills.''

''We see each other at the office. That's it.'' She hesitated, then added in what she hoped was a casual tone, ''But I was wondering something.''

''Oh?''

''Did Taylor come straight back to Port William after law school?''

Judging from Elsie's expression, she wasn't fooled by Zelda's casual air.

''No, indeed,'' she said. ''He went into practice over in Charleston, just like he always talked about doing.''

''Then how did he end up back here?''

Elsie hesitated, then shook her head. ''I can't say I know the whole story. Besides, that's something you'd best be asking him,'' she said.

It was a surprising display of discretion for a woman who loved to gossip. First Darlene, now Elsie. It appeared to Zelda if she stuck around Port

William long enough this time, the whole blasted town would reform.

"I can't ask my boss something like that," she said piously. "It's too personal."

Elsie winked. "I know. If you were just asking because he's your boss, I'd tell you what I do know. But you're looking for more than the bare facts, and that's something you ought to hear from him."

"Why does everybody act so mysterious about this?" she snapped impatiently. "It's not like I'm some scandalmonger from a tabloid. Taylor and I were close once."

"A lot of water's gone under the bridge since then, for both of you. Seems to me if you expect to be close again, you'd best open up those lines of communication."

Zelda scowled at her, then grinned at the common sense suggestion. Whatever else her flaws might be, Elsie Whittingham had always had good solid advice for a lonely girl who hadn't always trusted her own mother's slurred words of wisdom. "Okay, okay, you've made your point."

"Can I offer one more word of advice?"

"You're asking?" she said incredulously. "Would a *no* stop you?"

Elsie chuckled. "Not likely. Don't go stirring things up unless you've got a good reason for doing it. Taylor's had a rough time of it. He doesn't need someone else to come along and hurt him."

"What makes you think I could do anything to hurt Taylor?"

"Because, honey, you always could, and some things just flat-out never change."

All night long Elsie's warning seemed to reverberate in Zelda's head. Was it possible that Taylor did hold some deeply buried feelings for her, even after all this time? It would explain that unguarded expression she'd caught on his face, the hunger in that kiss.

If so, then, what right did she have stirring things up? Was she still hoping for revenge? Or were there feelings of her own, feelings that went beyond resentment, that she hadn't yet grappled with, that maybe she didn't want to face at all? Common sense told her to proceed with caution.

Of course, according to legend in Port William, anyway, common sense wasn't something Zelda Lane had ever given a hang about. Since she'd already been tarred with that particular brush, she couldn't see much reason to prove them wrong now.

The next day when Zelda placed a stack of letters on Taylor's desk, instead of beating a rapid retreat, she lingered. Seeing the tense set of his shoulders, she longed to stand behind him and massage away the ache. Given his overall attitude toward her, though, he'd probably charge her with assault. Maybe even attempted murder, if her fingers happened to skim his neck.

"I was surprised to find you living in Port William after all this time," she confessed in what she hoped was a casual tone.

He barely glanced at her. "Why? It's home."

Though his response was hardly an invitation for an intimate tête-à-tête, she sat down anyway. "But you were always so determined to live in Charleston or Columbia, and run for office."

He straightened and regarded her evenly. "I did live in Charleston, and I did run."

"You did?" she said, unable to hide her astonishment. If Taylor had run for office, why wasn't he in the capital now? He wasn't the kind of man who would even enter a race, unless he'd been virtually assured of winning.

"What happened?" she asked finally, since he didn't seem inclined to enlighten her on his own.

A dark look crossed his face. He drummed his fingers on his desk, then shoved them through his hair. The nervous ritual was familiar, but in the past she'd only seen him act that way around Beau, when he'd been struggling not to tell him off. She was absolutely certain now that he intended to toss her out without replying.

Instead, he merely glared at her impatiently, then bent back over his work. A wise woman would have taken the hint. Zelda, however, wasn't about to let it rest, now that she'd finally opened up the subject.

"Taylor?"

He looked up, scowling. "Damn it, I don't have time for this. I hired you to work, not to cross-examine me."

"I can't do the best possible job, if I don't really know the person for whom I'm working."

"You've known me for the better part of the past thirty years," he reminded her.

She shook her head. "I knew you ten years ago. You've changed, Taylor. You used to be just as big a risk-taker as me, maybe even more daring. Now you've settled for boring. I can't help but wonder why."

He tossed his pen aside. "Zelda, what's this really all about? I seriously doubt whether you're worried about how stodgy I've become. Besides, you're here on a temporary basis, right? Maybe for one more week. Less than a year, if you decide to fulfill the terms of your mother's will. I don't see much need to confess all my deep, dark secrets to you."

"Who better to talk to than an old friend who's leaving town?" she shot right back, angered by his assumption that she wouldn't last one instant beyond the year necessary to satisfy the terms of the will. "I'll take your secrets with me."

"How reassuring. I'll keep that in mind if I ever feel the need to make a confession."

Zelda groaned and barely resisted the urge to shake him. Or kiss him until he looked as bemused as he had at her house a few weeks back. "Why can't you stop being so evasive and just answer me? Is the truth so terrible? Maybe you could just start by telling me about Caitlin. In the past three weeks, you've never once mentioned her name."

A faint spark of warmth lit his eyes. "Seems to me you already know about her," he said dryly as he glanced pointedly at the framed picture on his desk.

"I know she exists," she corrected, refusing to be baited. "I don't know anything about her or about her mother."

"Frankly, I can't believe no one's filled you in," he muttered. His gaze narrowed suspiciously. "Or is that why you're asking, just so you can gloat?"

"Gloat about what? No one's told me a damn thing. In fact, everyone's so tight-lipped, you'd think I was asking about national security. If you don't want to talk about your marriage, then tell me about the election."

"Look it up in the local paper. There were plenty of stories at the time."

"I've worked for a highly publicized attorney in L.A. I know how the media can distort things. I'm asking for your version," she said with exaggerated patience.

Taylor uttered a sigh of resignation. "Damn it, you always were persistent," he grumbled.

She grinned, relaxing slightly. Victory was just within her grasp. She could sense it. She just had to reel him in. "Glad to know I haven't lost the knack for it. I'm still waiting for an answer, by the way."

"I lost, okay?" he said, then added with undisguised bitterness, "That ought to make you happy."

The words were curt, but it was the bleak expression in his eyes that distressed her. Taylor rarely showed signs of his vulnerabilities. Whatever had happened had hurt him deeply. With anyone else that might have dissuaded her from pursuing the topic, but she sensed that Taylor needed to talk. He wouldn't, unless she badgered him into it. So she kept at him, but her tone softened.

"Why would that make me happy?" she asked, genuinely puzzled by the comment. "I always wanted what was best for you. Remember when we used to talk about how we would redecorate the White House one day? I believed in that dream, Taylor. Even when I knew I wouldn't be the woman there with you, I still wanted you to get there someday."

"Sure," he said disbelievingly. "Once upon a time, maybe you felt that way, but I suspect I haven't exactly been in your prayers in recent years."

"Maybe, maybe not, but I do know how much being elected to public office meant to you and your family. In fact," she added dryly, "who would understand that better than I would? I paid a high enough price, so you could fulfill Beau's ambition."

"It was my ambition, Zelda, not just my father's, but you're right. It sure as hell did ruin things between us. The blame for that's as much mine as my father's."

Once again filled with regret, Zelda sighed. "It didn't have to ruin things for us, Taylor. I think that's what made me angriest. You bought into your father's assumption that I'd be a liability." She shook off the memories. It was too late now to change what had happened back then. "Look, all I'm saying is that I know how disappointed you must have been, but that still doesn't explain why you're here in Port William again. Losing a campaign wouldn't send you running back home."

He regarded her intently for the space of a heart-beat and then he sighed deeply. "No," he said quietly, "but losing my wife did."

Zelda felt as if the wind had been knocked out of her. "Losing your wife," she echoed in dismay. "How? Surely she didn't divorce you just because you lost an election."

"No. She died," he said bluntly.

The succinct reply explained a lot . . . and nothing at all. This time, though, Taylor's dark, forbidding gaze kept Zelda from pressing for more answers. But it didn't keep her from wondering.

After she'd left his office, Taylor felt all of the old pain and anguish wash over him. The wound, which had been healing nicely at long last, had been ripped open with just one sympathetic look from Zelda. He didn't want her sympathy. He didn't even want any-one to know how much pain he was in. He just wanted to be allowed to exist in peace. He wanted a life with no expectations and no bitter disappointments. No highs. No lows. With a woman like Zelda, there'd always be plenty of both. He shuddered at the thought.

Clearly, though, Zelda didn't intend to let him get off that easily. Just behind her sympathetic expression, he'd seen the familiar stubborn determination to probe until she knew everything. He'd remembered too late how persistent she could be and how perceptive. She'd guessed, when no one else ever had, how much he'd resented Beau's control of his life, even when they'd shared the same goals.

It was obvious, too, that Zelda blamed his father for everything that they'd lost. Some day he would have to correct that impression. In the end, it had been his mother who'd persuaded him to see reason, who'd gently pointed out how much more suitable a woman like Maribeth would be when he eventually ran for office. No one regretted the success of her persuasion more than his mother did today. He wondered if perhaps that was why she'd been so insistent that he help Ella Louise with her will, a gesture to make amends for a wrong done to Ella Louise's daughter.

Or maybe even a gesture meant to give him a second chance at happiness. What a laugh that was! He'd botched his life up royally and, bottom line, he had no one to blame but himself. He hadn't been an impressionable kid when he'd cut Zelda out of his life. He'd made choices, bad ones, and he was going to spend the rest of his miserable life paying for them. Wasn't that what penance was all about?

Taylor sighed as he struggled to face the fact that it was only a matter of time before Zelda heard the whole story about his marriage. He knew he should be the one to tell her, but the words just hadn't come. It had been easier to talk about the election. Losing a political race was one thing. Failure was another.

He admitted to himself that pride had kept him quiet. That and the fact that they both knew her presence here was only temporary. There was no point in sharing secrets, in allowing a touch of intimacy that could delude either of them that things could ever be the same between them. His decision to keep silent had been a good one, he told himself repeatedly.

If that were true, though, why was that gnawing turmoil in his stomach worse than ever? And why did he sense that he'd missed an ideal opportunity to strengthen a bond that never should have been broken in the first place?

He still hadn't answered those questions by Friday afternoon. At three that day, as he'd sworn to Ms. Patterson that he would do religiously once a month, he drove to the small private boarding school where he'd sent Caitlin. Ignoring his parents' objections, he'd told himself that he was no match for a precocious seven-year-old who needed rigid discipline. Except for those lonely hours in the evening, when he desperately missed the sound of Caitlin's laughter, he almost believed it.

He stood outside the gates and watched her come down the walkway in her blue and gray uniform, her wild black curls tamed into braids, her pace sedate. Something inside him wrenched at the sight, but he didn't dare admit to himself that he'd preferred the exuberant child who'd flung herself into his arms with sticky kisses only a year before.

"Hello, Daddy," she said in a soft, emotionless voice. Her eyes, the same gray as his own, were shadowed in a way no child's should be.

"Hey, puddin'. How's my best girl?" He tugged on a braid and a familiar, impish grin flitted too briefly across her face. "How's school?"

"It's okay. I got an A in math. My teacher says I have a very orderly mind."

Taylor winced. How could he ever have thought that such praise would delight him? It sounded so dull, so predictable. It sounded like something to be said once all the life had been squeezed out of a person, not words to be used to describe a seven-year-old.

Had seeing Zelda again reminded him of what it had been like to be a child? Before they'd met, he'd been every bit as studious and diligent as his daughter was now. Zelda had breathed the spirit back into him. What terrors they had been! For the first time in a very long time, he found himself smiling at the memories.

Caitlin regarded him curiously. "What's so funny, Daddy?"

The surprise written all over her face reminded him of how seldom he smiled these days. "I was just thinking back to a long time ago."

"About Mom?"

He felt as if the blood drained out of his face. "No," he said, trying to keep the edge out of his voice. "No, I wasn't thinking about your mother."

Caitlin's expression, which for one brief instant had been that of a happy, exuberant kid again, shut down immediately at his terse response.

Taylor cursed himself for his insensitivity. He'd vowed that he would never do anything to destroy the love Caitlin had felt for her mother, no matter how much he blamed Maribeth for ruining their lives. Obviously he was going to have to guard his words more closely.

During the drive back to Port William, he tried to put that spark back into her eyes with silly teasing, but Caitlin was too sensitive to his moods to respond. She was silent all the way, lost in thoughts. Looking at her sitting stiff and silent beside him came very close to breaking his heart.

## Chapter Seven

Zelda stood at the front window of the office long past six o'clock, watching for Taylor. Dusk settled in right along with anxiety over his likely reaction to her presence on his return. Still, she couldn't make herself go. She switched on the outside lights illuminating the driveway and waited.

Though he hadn't said a word about his destination, she knew from what Darlene had told her that he was probably going to pick up his daughter. Even knowing that he would be furious to find her still around, she had dragged out her work until it seemed silly not to stay just a little longer. She needed to see for herself the child she might have shared with Taylor if only things had been different, needed to try to understand the currently unfathomable dynamics of their father-daughter relationship.

She knew what she was doing was foolish, that it would be emotionally costly. Still, she stood there, gazing down the street, wondering how she dared to get involved. Once she'd left Port William, would she be able to bear thinking of that little girl going through life without a mother and banished by a father for reasons Zelda couldn't begin to comprehend? Wouldn't it be better not to know what Taylor's child was like, how much she needed to be loved?

Too late for caution now, she thought. Her heart began to hammer with anticipation as Taylor's car turned the corner. As he pulled into the driveway, her breath seemed to catch in her throat. Finally the car door opened and Caitlin emerged.

Instantly Zelda felt the tug on her heart, the sting of tears in her eyes. She wasn't sure what she'd expected, but it certainly wasn't this placid, too thin child who walked so sedately at her father's side instead of skipping ahead. She carried an expensive overnight bag rather than some outrageously colorful tote like the ones most youngsters preferred. So little, yet pretending to be so grown-up. Zelda's heart ached for her.

Picking up her own purse and firming her resolve, Zelda swiftly left the office, locking the door behind her. She met the pair on the walk, defiantly ignoring Taylor's forbidding expression. She hunkered down in front of Caitlin and held out her hand.

"Hi, I'm Zelda. I'm your dad's new secretary. I've been looking forward to meeting you."

Caitlin placed one delicate hand in Zelda's. "Hello," she said, her tone very proper, very reserved. "I'm pleased to meet you, too."

She glanced up at her father for approval. Then with an obvious flash of childish curiosity, she asked, "What kind of name is Zelda?"

"A troublesome one," Zelda admitted with a self-conscious laugh. "My mother happened to love a particular author and since she couldn't name me after him, she named me after his wife. When I was your age, I really hated my name. Now I don't mind it so much."

"You probably just got used to it," Caitlin said, displaying a wisdom beyond her years. Zelda couldn't help wondering how often the child had been told that she would get used to something eventually, just to be patient.

"Maybe I did get used to it," Zelda agreed. "Or maybe it was that someone used to say my name with so much love in his voice that it suddenly seemed very special." She could feel Taylor's gaze burning into her, but she refused to look at him.

"Your boyfriend?" Caitlin asked, obviously every bit as fascinated as she might have been by some gloriously romantic fairy tale.

Zelda glanced up at Taylor, then back at his daughter. "Yes. He was, back then."

"Did you marry him?" Caitlin inquired ingenuously.

Before Zelda could respond, Caitlin confided, "I'm going to marry a prince someday and live in a castle."

Zelda nodded seriously. "Now that seems like a very good goal to me," she replied approvingly. "Have you picked out the castle?"

Caitlin giggled. "No. I've never even seen one, but daddy promised to take me to. . ." She looked at her father. "What's that place you said you'd take me?"

"Europe," Taylor said, his lips twitching with amusement. "It's across the Atlantic Ocean. Remember, I showed you once on the globe."

"He showed me pictures of castles in a book, too," Caitlin confided to Zelda. "I think I liked the one at Disney World best."

Taylor laughed aloud at that. Something inside Zelda twisted free at the sound. How long had it been since she'd heard his laughter?

"Sweetheart, that wasn't Disney World," he said, his hand caressing his daughter's head. "That was Neuschwanstein in Germany. It was built by King Ludwig."

Caitlin wasn't impressed by the historical information. "Well, it looked like the one at Disney World. I see it all the time on TV." She inched a little closer to Zelda. "Maybe you'd like to stay for dinner and I could show you the castles, too. Do you know any princes?''

Zelda heard the hopeful note in her voice, but she also caught the dismayed expression on Taylor's face. Discretion called for polite excuses.

"Maybe another time," she promised. "Your dad probably already has other plans for tonight. I'm sure he wants to hear all about what you're doing at school. And I can be thinking about whether I've ever crossed paths with any princes."

"But I'm not home very much," Caitlin said wistfully, casting an appealing look up at her father. "It would by okay, wouldn't it, Daddy? Please."

Zelda saw Taylor's resolve wavering and knew that there was very little he would deny his daughter, no matter how hard he'd tried to distance himself from her by putting her out of sight in that boarding school. "If Zelda has the time, of course, she can stay," he conceded with undisguised reluctance.

Caitlin obviously wasn't aware of the subtle nuances between the adults. Her eyes lit up. "See. I told you it would be okay. You can stay, can't you?"

Zelda regarded Taylor intently. He gave a faint, albeit unhappy, nod. "I would love to stay," she told Caitlin, and meant it. She had been instantaneously charmed by this pint-size version of Taylor. A maternal instinct, long ago forced into dormancy, rebelliously reappeared.

As if she sensed that she'd found an ally, the child immediately tucked her hand into Zelda's and led her inside. "Maybe you can teach me to cook," she said. "Daddy's not very good."

"I know," Zelda said, casting a sly look at the indignant Taylor, who was scowling with feigned ferocity at his traitorous daughter. "Once he tried to make me a hamburger and burned it to a crisp."

What she neglected to say was that he'd been so busy kissing her, he hadn't given the hamburgers a second thought. It was clear from the heat that rose in Taylor's eyes that he remembered the incident every bit as clearly as she did, that he, too, recalled how her skin had heated beneath his touch, how her mouth had opened so readily beneath his. Now his gaze lingered on her face as if they could recapture the sweetness and passion of that moment without so much as a touch. Awareness shimmered through her, followed all too quickly by desire.

But even as her body hummed with longing, Taylor visibly composed himself. Through some supreme act of will that Zelda wished she could emulate, he replaced intensity with determined amusement.

"Perhaps if I hadn't been so distracted that night," he taunted, bringing a flush to Zelda's face as he ushered them into the kitchen. With one lasting knowing look cast in Zelda's direction, he grinned and said, "Now, sit down, you two, and let me prove how you've both misjudged me."

"Misjudged, hell," Zelda murmured, thinking that she'd had Taylor pegged almost as far back as she could remember. Too bad he didn't seem to know her at all. He'd pasted a label on her years ago and hadn't bothered to note that it was outdated.

"Daddy, maybe you should let Zelda cook," Caitlin insisted, regarding him worriedly as he stripped off his jacket and rolled up his sleeves.

Giving his daughter yet another indignant look, he tugged open the refrigerator and pulled a casserole from inside. With a deliberately dramatic flourish, he turned on the oven and popped the dish in. "See," he said triumphantly. "All done."

Hands on tiny hips, Caitlin made a face at her father. "Grandma made it, didn't she?" she guessed, then added with childish derision, "That's not cooking."

He winked at her. "Maybe not, but at least we know it'll be edible. Now, scoot, and put your things away. Let me talk to Zelda for a few minutes and catch up on what happened at the office after I left to pick you up."

Caitlin bounced off her chair and ran to the door. Then she hesitated and shot a worried look at Zelda. "You won't go, will you?"

"And miss this casserole your father has so expertly warmed up? Not a chance."

When Caitlin had gone, Zelda turned to Taylor. "I'm sorry she put you on the spot."

"Are you really?" he inquired skeptically. "We both know you'd probably finished your work a good hour before Caitlin and I got home."

She chafed under his knowing look. "Are you accusing me of engineering this meeting?"

"Yep."

She took heart from the fact that he didn't appear as angry as he might have been. "Okay, so what if I did?"

"Look, it has nothing to do with you personally, or even you and me," he insisted when she raised a skeptical brow. "Caitlin lost one person who was very important to her. I won't have her form an attachment to someone else who's only going to disappear from her life."

Zelda's indignation flared, then vanished in the space of a heartbeat. How could she argue with a warning that only stemmed from Taylor's obvious love and concern for his daughter? "I'll be careful, Taylor. I promise."

He sighed and shook his head. "Careful?" he echoed. "I didn't think the word was in your vocabulary."

It was something Beau Matthews might have said, Zelda thought as her temper began to flare. She'd spent the past three weeks practically standing on her head to prove to Taylor that she was no longer some impetuous, irresponsible kid. Obviously she hadn't made a dent in that thick skull of his.

Fueled by irritation and a sudden streak of pure mischief, she turned slowly and began moving toward him. Her pace was lazy, but relentless. He backed up a step, apparently warned by something he read in her expression that she was on the warpath and had no intention of playing fair.

"Zelda?"

"Don't worry, Taylor," she soothed. "This will be painless."

Alarm rose in his eyes. "What are you up to?"

"No good," she said cheerfully. "Isn't that what you usually expect from me?"

He backed into the counter. Zelda kept coming until her body was pressed against his, toe to toe, thigh to thigh, hips to . . . well, there was no doubt at all about what impact she was having on him. So, he wasn't nearly as immune as he pretended to be. Unfortunately, she thought as a shudder swept through her, neither was she. This game of hers could have dangerous consequences. Even knowing that, she wasn't about to stop.

Looking him straight in the eye, she braced her hands on his chest. She began to fiddle with the buttons on his shirt until the first four were undone and she could slide her fingers into the mat of crisp hairs on his chest. His skin blazed beneath her slow, tantalizing touch. She could feel the sudden racing of his heart, heard the sharp intake of breath as she provocatively skimmed a fingernail across one taut masculine nipple.

"Zelda, what the hell do you think you're doing?" he demanded in a choked whisper.

She noticed with a measure of satisfaction that for all of his protests, he wasn't trying very hard to escape. "If you don't know, then you've obviously been out of circulation for far too long."

He brushed at her hands, but the gesture lacked conviction. She simply laced her fingers together behind his neck and touched her lips to his feverish cheek, liking the way the rough stubble felt against her own softer skin. There was no mistaking the shudder that swept through him or the desire that darkened his eyes. She pressed a kiss on the opposite cheek, then another on his furrowed brow. Then, when his breath was coming in ragged gasps, she began the same slow, deliberately provocative pattern all over again.

"Zelda? Why are you doing this?"

"Just living up to expectations," she replied innocently as she skimmed a finger across his mouth, tracing the outline of his lips.

"Expectations?" he echoed weakly.

"Sure. I'm still wicked, untamed Zelda Lane, right? Daughter of the town's most eccentric lady." She emphasized her words with a slow, deep kiss that left them both trembling. She nodded in satisfaction. This was working out rather nicely. She was enjoying herself. So was Taylor, if his dazed expression was anything to judge by. Just to make sure he didn't get to thinking too hard about what was happening, she kissed him again, molding her mouth to his, teasing his lips with her tongue until the whole world tilted.

When she could finally manage to speak again, she added nonchalantly, "Might as well enjoy myself, right?"

As bemused as he was, as badly as his traitorous body ached for her, Taylor couldn't ignore the sad, wistful note in her voice. There was a lot of hurt behind that jaunty comment, a hurt he didn't begin to understand, but which touched him deeply just the same.

It also made him feel like a heel for allowing her to go on this way, *for enjoying it, damn it!* He admitted the latter to himself only after some deep and troublesome soul-searching. He was tempted, all right, tempted to play this scene straight through to the end.

Only the knowledge that they would both hate themselves in the morning—and Caitlin's inconvenient presence in another part of the house—kept him from giving in to the wild sensations Zelda's determined touches were arousing in him. He put his hands on her waist and lifted her away, putting a much needed inch or two of space between them. No more, he noticed ruefully. He could still feel the heat radiating from her, still catch a whiff of some subtle, exotic fragrance.

Ignoring the rebellious glint in her eyes, he smoothed her hair back from her face with one hand. He caressed the pale shadows under her eyes, traced the outline of her kiss-swollen lips with his thumb.

"I'm sorry," he said finally.

She regarded him with obvious bewilderment. "Sorry? For what?"

"Because you've been trying so hard for weeks now to prove what a changed woman you are, and I obviously haven't been paying attention. That's what this seduction ritual is all about, isn't it?"

She regarded him with feigned astonishment. "Well, hallelujah! I'm so glad something finally got through that incredibly thick skull of yours. What was it? The kiss? That certainly couldn't have been it. You were definitely afraid I was about to have my wicked way with you."

"Was not," he said, unable to resist being drawn into the argument. The desire to laugh with sheer exhilaration shimmered just beneath the surface. Terrified of giving in to it, of succumbing to Zelda's seductive ways, he choked back his amusement.

"Were, too," she taunted right back. "I dare you to kiss me back."

Mustering every bit of self-restraint he could, he gave her an impersonal peck on the cheek. A quick, hit-and-run kind of kiss. A meaningless kiss. So meaningless he almost couldn't stop himself.

"Be careful what you ask for, you wicked little she-devil. You could get it," he warned.

Zelda sighed so heavily it almost broke his heart. "Not me, Taylor," she said in a way that expressed resigned acceptance rather than self-pity. "For some of us, nothing comes easy. They tell me it builds character."

For Taylor, who'd learned all about struggling only after years of feeling blessed, the lesson had done just that. He was a stronger man today than he had been when he'd allowed his father to drive Zelda out of his life. Strong enough to say no to temptation. He couldn't help thinking, though, that it was too bad that the lesson had come too late for the two of them.

"Be grateful you learned how to fight back at such an early age," he told her. "You had more character at fourteen than I did ten years ago when I let you go. I think maybe you've always known exactly who you are and what you wanted out of life. I'm just finding out about myself. I'm not so sure I like what I'm discovering."

He turned away and busied himself getting the silverware for the table. Zelda's hesitant hand on his shoulder sent a wave of pure longing washing through him, a longing for something as real and normal as a wife and home, nights like this with their teasing intimacy.

He glanced back at her and saw that she was regarding him quizzically. Because he didn't want her fussing over him or asking a lot of unanswerable questions, he met that inquisitive gaze with a defiant look.

"Don't go making anything out of that," he warned.

His sharp tone didn't seem to faze her, however. Her gaze never wavered.

"Don't be too hard on yourself, Taylor," she scolded. "Remember, you're still the man I fell in love with. Anyone who could capture Zelda Lane's hard heart couldn't be all bad, now could they?"

He was prevented from answering by Caitlin's noisy arrival. It was just as well, he told himself. He'd had no idea what to say, what Zelda had expected him to say. Just as he was trying to puzzle out the answer to that, he heard Caitlin's dismayed yelp, followed almost immediately by Zelda's unrestrained hoot of laughter.

Glancing their way, he groaned at the sight that greeted him.

"Daddy," Caitlin scolded, "you burned dinner again."

Zelda winked at him. "Habit, I guess."

## Chapter Eight

Taylor grabbed a pot holder and snatched the smoldering casserole from the oven. "It's just a little crisp around the edges," he informed them, fanning aside the smoke.

Zelda peered over his shoulder, the exotic scent of her perfume counterpointed by the aroma of burned noodles. "Crisp?" she repeated. "Quite an understatement, I'd say."

"It's still edible," Taylor insisted.

"I don't want any," his traitorous daughter insisted. "It's yucky."

Taylor refused to meet Zelda's gaze. Given how the dish had wound up in its charred state, he could just imagine the sparks of tolerant I-told-you-so amusement lighting her eyes.

"Okay, I'll put a frozen pizza in for you," he told Caitlin. "Zelda, how about you? Pizza or some of this delicious casserole."

Caitlin regarded their guest expectantly.

"Your mother didn't know I'd be here when she sent this over, right?" Zelda inquired.

His gaze narrowed suspiciously. "Right," he agreed. "So, what's your point?"

"Then I suppose I could risk the casserole," she said thoughtfully. "Surely a little charcoal won't poison me, and I wouldn't want to do anything to undermine your masculine pride."

He shot her a wry look. "Very funny. My ego doesn't need any mercy stroking by you."

That devilish glint immediately rose in her eyes. "Oh, really?" she said softly.

He cast a warning look in Caitlin's direction. His daughter, however, seemed oblivious to the innuendos. She'd climbed on a chair, removed a pizza from the freezer and already had it on a baking sheet. It was all too obvious that it was a routine they'd been through before. Taylor avoided looking at Zelda as he took the pizza from Caitlin, put it in the oven and turned up the heat.

"I'll watch it, Daddy," she informed him.

Zelda shot her a conspiratorial grin. "I think that's probably a very good idea, Caitlin. Your father seems to be easily distracted tonight."

Taylor couldn't think of a single response he could utter with his impressionable daughter in the room. It didn't prevent him from regarding Zelda in a way that promised very sweet revenge for her sassy tongue. He hadn't looked forward to anything so much in ages, a fact that scared the daylights out of him.

Zelda spent Saturday having another long talk with herself. It was getting to be a disconcerting habit. Pretty soon she'd be surrounded by cats and acting like a slightly dotty old spinster.

Still, she had things to work out. After Friday night she knew that she was treading on dangerous turf. Coming back to Port William had stirred up old longings.

She picked up one of her mother's favorite books, *This Side of Paradise,* and clung to it, rubbing her fingers over the worn cover.

"Oh, Mama, what should I do?" she murmured.

She was beginning to get an inkling that this turmoil was part of her mother's plan. Maybe Ella Louise had recognized that too many things had been left unresolved when Zelda fled to Los Angeles with her heart in tatters. Maybe she'd known, as Zelda hadn't until the night before, that she'd never be able to get on with her life in L.A. or in Port William until she'd dealt once and for all with the permanent ache Taylor Matthews had left inside her.

But a whole year? She'd barely been home a month and already things were more complicated, instead of less. Another eleven months and she probably wouldn't have a strand of hair left in her head with the way Taylor's impossible ways made her want to tear it out.

Okay, this wasn't something she could blame entirely on Taylor. These were her emotions. Stupid, wasted emotions, as near as she could tell. Just because he'd kissed her as though he'd meant it didn't prove he was about to get tangled up in something more lasting.

Go or stay? Stay or go? The choice tormented her for the rest of Saturday and all through the endless night.

On Sunday morning, with the memory of the challenge in Taylor's eyes on Friday still very much on her mind and Saturday's uncertainty even fresher, Zelda went to church. Sheer instinct had her up and dressed in a subdued silk dress before she considered the ramifications of showing up in a place where she was bound to run into Taylor's parents. Besides, it had been so long since she'd been inside a church, she ought to be praying that the rafters wouldn't collapse.

The minister, if it was still Jesse Hall, would probably offer up a few prayers of his own at the sight of her. He'd once had to call the volunteer fire department to drag her and Taylor down from the steeple. Not satisfied to ring the bell by pulling the rope, they'd climbed all the way up to give it a push or two at close range. The memory of Beau's horrified expression as he'd watched their undignified descent to the ground brought out a smile.

As she strolled across the lawn in front of the Port William Methodist Church, she glanced up at the steeple and felt an old familiar urge to do something outrageous. Maturity kept her feet planted firmly on the ground. Or so she told herself.

She nodded politely at half a dozen acquaintances. She couldn't help noticing the wary looks some of the women cast first at her and then at their husbands. Wanda Sue Oglethorpe actually latched possessively onto her husband's elbow and spun him around as if she feared that a simple nod in Zelda's direction might turn the man into a pillar of salt. Given Denny Oglethorpe's preference for bib overalls, flannel shirts and chewing tobacco, Zelda could have reassured Wanda Sue that she was welcome to him, if only the woman had asked.

Trying hard not to let the general lack of welcome bother her, Zelda made it as far as the door of the church before she heard her name called with anything resembling enthusiasm. She turned around just in time to see Caitlin running toward her, her face alight with pleasure.

"Well, good morning," she said, forcing herself not to look beyond the child for the father she was sure couldn't be far away. "Don't you look pretty?"

"Thank you," Caitlin said primly. "My grandmother bought this dress for me."

That didn't especially surprise Zelda. The gray wool dress with its simple white collar was precisely the choice she would have expected from Geraldine Matthews. Expensive and tasteful, it had about as much personality as oatmeal.

"I like yours better," Caitlin confided. "I wish I had a dress that color. What's it called?"

"Teal," Zelda said. "That's a shade of blue."

"Like your eyes, sort of." She spotted her father and ran to grab his hand and drag him over. "Look, Daddy, isn't Zelda's dress beautiful? It's called teal. Do you think I could have one that color?"

To Zelda's amusement, Taylor looked thoroughly bewildered. A typical male, she surmised.

"You have an entire closetful of clothes," he said finally. "Surely you already have something blue."

Caitlin regarded him impatiently. "Not blue, Daddy. Teal."

"We could find some material and make you one," Zelda offered. "If your father wouldn't mind."

"Please, Daddy," Caitlin implored. "I could wear it to my birthday party."

A sudden, indulgent twinkle lit his eyes. "Are you having a birthday party?" he teased.

"Next month. Remember? You promised. Grandmother said she'd bake a cake. And you said

I could bring some of my friends from school home for the whole weekend.''

"Is that next month? I could have sworn your birthday wasn't for ages yet."

A grin broke across Caitlin's too solemn face. "You're teasing me, aren't you? You remembered."

Taylor smiled. "Yes, I remembered. How could I possibly forget such an important occasion? As for a new dress, I suppose I could take you shopping for one." He looked as if he'd rather spend a month in jail.

"I'd really enjoy making one for her," Zelda offered again, not entirely certain why she was so hellbent on insinuating herself into Taylor's life. Perhaps it was the forlorn, lost look she saw so often in Caitlin's eyes. Perhaps it was merely her own need to experience what family life with Taylor might have been like, even if it was only for a few hours of pure make-believe.

"It wouldn't be any trouble," she insisted when she saw him wavering. "I could pick her up one afternoon to go look for material, then drive her back to school. My mother's sewing machine still works. I used it just the other day to make some curtains for the bedroom."

"Please," Caitlin said again. Wide blue eyes regarded her father with wistfulness.

In the end, Taylor was clearly no match for his daughter's appeal. He smiled. "I suppose it would be all right. I'll speak to the headmistress when I take

Caitlin back tomorrow. Then you'll be able to make the arrangements with her whenever it's convenient for you to drive over."

Caitlin flung herself into her father's arms. "Thank you. Thank you. Thank you." She grinned at Zelda. "It'll be so much fun. Maybe we can even go for ice cream after."

"Oh, I think ice cream would be an absolute necessity after a long afternoon of shopping."

Just then Caitlin caught sight of her grandparents and went running to tell them her news. Zelda's breath caught in her throat as she saw Geraldine Matthews shoot a questioning look in her direction. Beau Matthews looked thunderstruck. An instant later he was striding in their direction, his expression stormy.

Zelda stood her ground. Taylor didn't budge from where he stood next to her. The air around them seemed to crackle with sudden tension.

"Good morning, Father," he said.

"Damn it all," Beau thundered, glowering at Zelda.

Before he could launch into an embarrassing tirade, Taylor interceded. "You're standing on the church steps, Father, with all the neighbors listening to every word. Don't you think a little discretion is called for?" he said mildly.

A dull red flush crept up Beau's neck as he bit back whatever he'd been about to say. "We don't need the likes of you back in this town," he said in a low growl meant only for Zelda's ears.

"Dad! That kind of talk is uncalled for," Taylor said, his own tone furious. In a deliberate gesture of defiance, he put his hand protectively on Zelda's waist. He glanced down at her, his gaze filled with compassion. "I think we should be going inside now."

Zelda fought to blink back the sudden onset of tears. Damn it, the last thing she wanted was this man's pity. "Taylor, you don't need to do this."

"Yes," he said flatly, squaring his shoulders defiantly. "I do." He looked toward his mother, who'd remained a discreet distance away to prevent his daughter from overhearing whatever his father was likely to blurt out. "Caitlin, let's go inside now."

She scampered immediately to his side and tucked one hand into his, the other into Zelda's. Zelda felt her heart lurch at the unexpected display of solidarity. Together, ignoring Beau's furious oath and his wife's attempt to placate him, they walked inside and made their way to a pew at the front of the church.

It wasn't much of a triumph. Zelda knew that sooner or later she'd pay a price for it. An angered Beau Matthews was always a formidable enemy. Worse, she knew that by the end of the day word that Taylor had chosen her over his family would be all over Port William. The news would be dissected with almost the same surgical precision as the chicken at most Sunday dinners. Sides would be chosen. Bets would be placed. And once again, the romance of Zelda Lane and Taylor Matthews would be the hottest topic in town.

It was late Monday afternoon before Zelda had a chance to discuss with Taylor privately what had happened at church and its likely aftermath. Even then she hesitated to bring it up. She didn't want him denying as meaningless something that had meant so much to her. That stance made up in some small way for his failure to stick by her years ago.

She stood in the doorway to his office, watching as he bent over his law books, exhaustion evident in the weary set of his shoulders. She longed to have the right to massage away the tension, just to have the right to touch him at all in a way that wasn't sexual. Sometimes, if she allowed herself to think about it, it cut right through to her soul that he would tolerate an intimate caress, but refused any pretense of real caring. It reminded her all too clearly that he still thought of her as a woman whose morals were no better than they had to be.

And yet he had stood up to his father in public the day before, she thought with a faint stirring of hope. She had to know why he had been willing to risk all the speculation and potential embarrassment.

"Taylor?" she said finally.

He glanced up at her, his expression wary. "Yes?"

"Do you have a minute?"

"I'm right in the middle of researching the precedent on this case."

"I'll help you do that," she volunteered. "It won't take long."

"That's not your job," he protested.

"Maybe it's not exactly what you hired me to do, but I'm qualified as a paralegal. You might as well take advantage of all of my skills."

An unexpected spark of mischief danced in his eyes and made her heart flip over.

"All of them?" he taunted.

"You know what I meant." She drew in a deep breath. "Taylor, there's something I need to ask you."

As if he sensed that she was about to bring up a subject he didn't want to hear, he nodded with obvious reluctance. "Go ahead. Ask."

"Why did you do what you did yesterday? Why did you defend me to your father?"

"It was nothing."

"It was, and you know it. So did everyone else on the church lawn. I need to know why."

"Because I refuse to allow him to humiliate you like that. You've done nothing to deserve it."

"I hadn't done anything to deserve it ten years ago, either," she reminded him.

He sighed and rubbed his eyes. "I know that. But ten years ago, I wasn't very wise or very brave. I was single-minded and ambitious, and I thought my family knew what was best.'' He leveled his gaze on her. ''I regret that more than I can ever tell you.''

There was no mistaking the genuine anguish in his voice, the regret in his eyes, the absolute sincerity in his voice. It might have been the first genuinely honest thing he'd said to her in years.

''Maybe it's time to put the past behind us,'' she told him, her voice little more than a whisper. Now, just maybe they could move on. She realized that as hard as she'd been fighting it, that was what she wanted more than anything else in the world.

He nodded at her suggestion. ''It's probably way past time to do that,'' he agreed.

Her heart leapt, then crashed as she saw the expression in his eyes. Suddenly she recognized the *but* she should have heard in his voice. He struggled with it, then clearly lost the internal debate.

''But, Zelda . . .'' He hesitated again.

''What?'' she demanded impatiently. Whatever his reservations were, she wanted him to spell them out. She couldn't fight something that remained unspoken.

''I need to be honest with you.''

A sense of dread welled up inside her. Those were the kind of words always spoken before bad news, before rejection. He'd said the exact same words ten years before, though his voice had been shaking then, had lacked the conviction she'd just heard. Unable to encourage him to continue, after all, she simply waited, wishing there was more of a hint of turmoil in his eyes.

"I wouldn't want you thinking that meant we have a future," he said finally. "Or even a present."

An icy knot formed in the middle of Zelda's chest at his flat, unequivocal tone. In the end, the apology had been his way of closing a door, not opening one.

"No, of course not," she said around the lump in her throat.

And then, because she didn't think she could bear it another minute, she fled.

An hour later she was cursing herself for not telling him that she wasn't looking for anything from him, for not salvaging some tiny shred of pride by laughing in his face.

"Who needs you, Taylor Matthews?" That was what she should have said. "Who wants you?"

The problem, unfortunately, was that the answer to both questions seemed to be that she did. Ten years of separation and festering anger had not done a damn thing to dim the needing or the wanting. If she were very wise, if she had an ounce of pride left, she would walk in tomorrow morning and hand in her notice. The month's trial was ending, anyway. She could claim she missed Los Angeles more than she'd expected, that the estate meant nothing to her, and that a writer's scholarship in her mother's memory would be for the best. She could do that. She should.

But she knew in her heart that she wouldn't. She was going to stay in Port William and play this damnable charade out to the end. No matter how it turned out. No matter how much it hurt. Because this time she would not take the coward's way out and run. She would stay and fight for the man she loved as she should have ten years before.

## Chapter Nine

Zelda was slapping a fresh coat of paint on the outside of the house when she heard the muffled laughter behind her. Whirling around, she saw Sarah Lynn, her face alight with barely concealed mirth.

"Interesting color," she observed. "You trying to make a statement or what?"

Zelda regarded her indignantly. "There is nothing wrong with raspberry."

"For fruit, maybe even kitchen curtains, but a whole house? Can't say I've ever seen one that exact shade."

Zelda stepped back and studied the house intently. It was bright, somewhere between the color of cotton candy and actual ripe berries. With white trim, it ought to look downright cheerful. "I like it," she said staunchly.

"I take it, then, that you aren't planning to sell it, after all."

Zelda's gaze narrowed. Going or staying wasn't something she was prepared to commit to aloud. "Why would you say that?"

"Because you'd be painting it a nice subdued white if you hoped to find a buyer."

Zelda grimaced at Sarah Lynn's perceptiveness. "Okay, I'm painting it raspberry because I like raspberry," she conceded cautiously. "It's a happy color."

"And it'll drive Beau Matthews crazy every time he has to ride past this place."

Zelda grinned unrepentantly. "That, too."

"Has Taylor seen it?"

"No. I don't expect him to be dropping by anytime soon, not after what happened the last time he was here. In fact, I doubt he'd come into the office if he could help it."

Sarah Lynn settled into a rocking chair with an expectant look on her face. "Sounds fascinating."

"Don't look at me like that," Zelda chided. "I don't kiss and tell."

Sarah Lynn nodded as if she'd revealed every detail of a torrid love scene. "That would explain his behavior on the church lawn Sunday morning."

"You weren't even there."

"Didn't need to be. I had three phone calls by noon. The accounts were generally the same. Beau expressed his disapproval of your presence in Port William and Taylor told him off. Then, with his daddy about ready to explode, Taylor and Caitlin defied him and went inside with you. Accurate?"

"Close enough."

Sarah Lynn nodded in satisfaction. "I knew that boy'd wake up one of these days. Has he asked you to stay here permanently, yet?"

"Hardly. Offhand, I'd say this little display was nothing more than a belated rebellion on Taylor's part. I don't think it had much to do with me."

"Honey, it had everything to do with you. It's been eating away at Taylor for ten years the way he mistreated you back then, whether he wants to admit it or not. He still loves you. Always did. Always will."

Zelda shrugged. "I wish I could believe that, but I don't think so. I think he considers Sunday's act the ultimate apology. My guess is that he'd be perfectly happy if I skedaddled out of town so he wouldn't have to take another stance like that."

"I'm not sure who you're selling short here, yourself or Taylor. You're a woman any man would be proud to marry. And Taylor might have been a little misguided once upon a time, but he's a decent, honorable man, to say nothing of being a certified hunk who's aged like vintage wine."

"I'm not selling either of us short. I've developed a fair amount of self-confidence over the past ten years. And nobody ever knew Taylor's attributes better than I. They've kept me awake more nights than I care to admit to."

"Then what are you worrying about? It's just a matter of time before you all work things out. Some things in life are just meant to go together. Ham and eggs. Coffee and cream. You and Taylor."

Zelda regarded her wryly. "Do you know how many people no longer eat ham *and* eggs? Do you know how many take their coffee black? I think you've overestimated the certainties in life."

"Give it time, hon."

Zelda shook her head. "No. He flat-out told me not to read anything into what he did. What's past is past. We have no present and no future. He was adamant about that," she said, turning away so Sarah Lynn wouldn't see the tears that automatically sprang up as she repeated Taylor's words. She rubbed at her eyes with the backs of her paint-spattered fists, probably leaving streaks of raspberry down her face so she looked like a sad-faced clown.

Sarah Lynn uttered an unladylike sniff of derision. "Sounds an awful lot like a fool who's protesting too much. Did you believe him?"

"He wants me to," Zelda said firmly.

"Did you believe him?" Sarah Lynn repeated.

Zelda scowled at her. "I'm painting this damned house, aren't I?"

Sarah Lynn nodded in satisfaction. "Good. Just remember that sometimes a woman knows what's good for a man a lot sooner than he recognizes it. With Taylor, there's a whole lot of history to overcome."

"He says that's behind us."

"I'm not talking about your history with him, hon. Hell, one of these days he'll see that you were the best thing that ever happened to him. It's his marriage he has to get beyond. No one around here knows all the details, but Maribeth's death left Taylor with a lot of pain and bitterness. He's not over it yet."

"I'm not sure I want to get into a competition with the ghost of the undying love of his life."

"I don't think that's something you need to worry yourself about. To my knowledge, you're the first and only woman ever to get a rise out of him, including that so-called society woman he married. Taylor's a calendar-worthy hunk. A lot of women have tried to comfort him or straight-out seduce him, before, during and after his marriage. Since his wife's death, none have succeeded, so far as I know. He's always polite, but disinterested. He needs you, hon, needs you to put some joy back into his life. Maybe even more than you need him."

With that enigmatic declaration, Sarah Lynn hefted herself out of the rocker and headed for home. After she was gone, Zelda tried desperately to convince herself that Sarah Lynn was right, that staying in Port William and fighting for Taylor wasn't going to be the costliest mistake of her life.

Whether it was or it wasn't didn't seem to matter in the end. She might not have admitted it to Sarah Lynn, but she was staying for as long as it took and that was that.

Taylor studied the calendar on his desk and tried not to count backward to the first day Zelda had come to work for him. He didn't need to finish to know that she'd been there one month. Four weeks. All she'd committed to. It wouldn't surprise him to discover that she'd flown back to Los Angeles over the weekend. No one in Port William, least of all him, had exactly made her feel welcome. In fact, it would take a tough hide to withstand the insults his father alone had uttered.

One thing that Taylor knew, though few others did, was that Zelda's very attractive hide barely protected her vulnerabilities. She might have a smart mouth and daring ways, but underneath it all she still bore all the hurts of a kid who'd only wanted to fit in and somehow never had.

But if Ella Louise's eccentricities had caused her pain, they had also given her strength. No one would ever see Zelda Lane looking defeated; no one would ever guess how difficult things had been for her.

Except Taylor. And he had only made things worse. Damn, a man could hate himself for a mistake like that.

He glanced at his watch, then at the door. It was five before eight. Zelda was always at her desk on the dot of eight o'clock. Other people in Port William might be lax about opening and closing their offices, but she was always prompt. He watched the sweep of his second hand as it went around once, then twice, then a third time. To his deep regret, his heart seemed to thud with anxiety. What if she had gone? How would he feel about that?

The quiet opening and closing of the outside door kept him from having to be honest with himself. Even so, he couldn't deny the relief that washed over him as he heard her call out.

"Taylor, are you here already?" She poked her head into his office, obviously startled to find him behind his desk rather than at Sarah Lynn's where he could usually be found until eight-thirty, sometimes nine.

"Thought I'd get an early start today," he said. "I wasn't sure you'd be in."

"Why wouldn't I be?" she inquired.

"The month is up," he reminded her, "and we didn't discuss how you felt about staying on."

She grinned in a way that made his blood pump harder. It was a smug, savvy look that told him she knew things that he didn't, like maybe the feelings he hadn't wanted to admit to. She'd had that same look on her face the night they'd made love for the first time, within minutes of his firm vow that he would not, under any circumstances, touch her. She had a way of testing a man's resolve.

"Taylor, you're not shy about expressing your likes and dislikes," she said. "I figured if you weren't satisfied with my work, you'd have fired me before now, deal or no deal. As for me, if I'd intended to quit, I'd have told you."

"So you're staying on?" he said, trying not to sound too concerned about the answer.

"Looks that way," she said cheerfully. "Any problem with that?"

There was a daring glint in her eyes that worried him, but he wasn't about to question her motives. She was staying and, for the moment, God help him, that was enough.

"There is one thing I ought to warn you about, though," he said. "My father's coming by this morning. He insisted on meeting here, rather than out at the house."

He considered suggesting she might want to take the morning to go over to Caitlin's school, maybe take his daughter on that shopping spree, but something in her instantly forbidding expression told him he ought to keep that idea to himself.

"Should I send him straight in when he arrives?" she inquired in a crisp, all-business tone she'd probably acquired working for that fancy divorce lawyer in L.A.

Since she obviously considered herself equal to the task of sending his father anywhere, Taylor decided not to question how she intended to pull that off. "That would be fine."

"Will you need me to take notes?"

Taylor almost grinned at the thought of his father's reaction to having Zelda sit in on their private discussion. He decided not to press his luck. "I think I can handle it."

"You're the boss."

She said it so agreeably, Taylor couldn't quite figure out why he thought the tables in the office had been deftly turned and that Zelda Lane was definitely the one in charge.

The same thought struck him again later—along with astonishment and admiration—as he heard her cheerfully greet his father as if he were any other client dropping by for an appointment.

"Taylor's waiting for you," she said. "Go right on in and I'll bring along a cup of coffee. How would you like it? Black? Cream and sugar?"

Taylor's anxiety rose when he couldn't hear his father's reply. Had he had a heart attack at discovering that Zelda was working for his son? Surely he'd heard about that, though Taylor had skirted any mention of it himself. Perhaps he was busy strangling her, Taylor thought, and strode across his office, prepared to intercede.

He discovered his father staring at Zelda with open-mouthed astonishment. He couldn't really blame him. She did look like a different woman in that trim, navy blue power suit with its expensive gold trim. She'd even taken time in the past half hour to twist her auburn hair into some sort of severe style he'd never seen her wear before.

Taylor took an immediate dislike to the prim style. He had an almost irresistible urge to yank out every one of the pins holding it until it tumbled free again into the sexy style he preferred. As for the suits, he was getting sick of those, as well. He liked her better in bright colors and slinky fabrics, material that clung and molded and tempted.

Still, he couldn't help admiring her for trying to create a professional image that even her most judgmental critic couldn't quarrel with. Unfortunately, Beau didn't seem too receptive to the changes.

"Dad?" Taylor said softly.

His father pivoted slowly in his direction. "Have you gone and lost your mind, son?" He didn't bother to lower his voice when he said it.

Taylor saw Zelda's hands clench, even though her expression remained unwaveringly calm. Anger and resentment cut into him at his father's deliberate rudeness.

"Why is this woman here?" his father demanded.

"She works for me, and I'm damned lucky to have her," Taylor said coldly, moving a protective step closer to the woman in question. "Now, did you want to discuss some business with me, or did you drop in to try and tell me how to run my office? If so, you can leave now."

Apparently his father heard the finality in his tone, because his shoulders sagged in defeat. "I'll never understand you, boy," he said wearily. "You'd think you'd have learned something after that lunatic wife of yours all but ruined you and your chances at being elected anything but dogcatcher in this state."

At the harsh mention of Maribeth, a cold fury washed through Taylor. "Dad, that's enough! I think maybe we'd better get together some other time. Better yet, maybe you ought to take your legal affairs over to a lawyer in Charleston. I'm sure you can find one there who'd meet your high moral standards. I'm sick to death of trying."

With the bitter words still hanging heavily in the air, Taylor whirled and went back into his office, slamming the door behind him. A moment later the outer door slammed shut, practically shaking the whole structure. Then, as he'd expected, Zelda was in the doorway.

"What was that all about?" she asked quietly.

"That was something that's been building up for a lifetime. I'm sorry you had to witness it."

"You hurt him, you know."

He regarded her wryly. "That's a twist, you feeling sorry for my father."

She shrugged. "Surprised the hell out of me, too. But the look in his eyes... Taylor, whatever he's done, it's only because he wanted what was best for you."

"You know how that road to hell got paved."

"With good intentions. Look, I've always been an easy target for Beau's frustration and, believe me, I haven't liked it, but I never doubted his love for you. Some people just don't recognize that sometimes loving means letting go, letting a person make his own mistakes."

Taylor shook his head impatiently. "Zelda, you're only the tip of the iceberg. My father's always wanted to control my life. He handpicked Maribeth for me. Now he blames me because the marriage didn't turn out the way he wanted it to. It wasn't my fault. It wasn't his fault. Hell, it probably wasn't even Maribeth's fault."

"What happened?"

"She died. I told you that."

"Taylor, I can see that there's more to it than that. Your father said the marriage ruined you and your chances at public office. Whatever happened, it's eating away at you."

"I don't see any point in talking about it," he insisted stubbornly. "It won't change anything."

Zelda stepped closer and propped herself on the edge of his desk so that their knees were touching. "Taylor."

She said it with such quiet insistence that he was forced to meet her gaze or admit that he was a coward. He refused to do that. He looked into those clear turquoise eyes of hers and saw the need to understand, the compassion that was available just for the asking.

"What happened?" she prodded.

The question hovered in the air, daring him to respond. Drawn by a force he couldn't ignore, Taylor slowly stood and reached for her. It was an instinctive, needy action, and he suspected he was going to be furious with himself a few minutes from now. He told himself he didn't need the compassion or the understanding, but he wouldn't deny the need for Zelda. It had always been a part of him, like the unruly curl of his hair or the beating of his heart.

As he pulled her into the circle of his embrace, one hand moved instinctively to her hair, seeking the pins and withdrawing them one by one. As they dropped to the floor, curls tumbled loose to skim her shoulders and flow like silk over his fingers. Some mysterious, seductive scent was released, as well, surrounding them.

"Your hair's so soft," he told her, his voice a husky whisper. "Don't ever pin it up like that again."

"I wanted to look professional for your father."

"Not necessary." He heard the catch in her breath as he skimmed her cheek with his fingers, reveled in the quick little flutter of her pulse. "You could ditch the prim little suits, too."

A flash of mischief sparked in her eyes. "Now?" she said, reaching immediately for the top button of her jacket.

A groan sprang loose from deep inside him. He'd forgotten just how quick she was to respond to any sort of dare. Or maybe he hadn't.

"Dear heaven, no," he protested a little too vehemently, though a part of him prayed she wouldn't listen. She had always been able to tempt him beyond reason, to make his breath lodge in his throat and his pulse race even as he tried his very best to cling to sanity. She was doing it again.

"Just one button," she taunted, sliding one gold circle through its confining hole. The sedate fabric separated an indiscreet inch, just enough to tantalize, just enough to make his heart hammer with anticipation.

"Zelda." It was an undeniable moan, not the sort of warning anyone would have taken seriously, least of all a woman like Zelda.

Instead of reaching for another of her own buttons, though, she began to dabble with his. Eyes sparkling with devilment stayed locked with his. She slipped her fingers inside his shirt, her nails skimming his chest in a gesture he could see was meant to be deliberately provocative. His whole body ached with the effort of trying to hide his response. Some things, however, couldn't be hidden and Zelda knew, she *knew*, that it wouldn't take much and he would be lost. They'd be making love on top of his desk, on the floor of his office, maybe both, before they were done. He wondered a little breathlessly if she'd dare, if he had the will left to stop her.

"Zelda, anyone could walk in at any second," he protested.

She grinned unrepentantly. "Exciting, isn't it?"

As a matter of fact, it was, but he could see that admitting to that would not slow things down. The woman was a danger junkie. She was already fiddling with his belt buckle, an action that made his blood pump harder and faster than a new strike in a Texas oil field.

Finally, reluctantly, with one ragged, indrawn breath, he reclaimed sanity the way an honorable, upright pillar of the community was supposed to. This wasn't the time or the place. Nor was his hurting and their desire any reason to break a long-standing vow to keep his life on a steady, uneventful course. He'd had all the passion, all the unexpectedness, he could stand for one lifetime. Zelda promised more of both.

"I—I have a meeting," he said, struggling with the lie.

"Where?" she inquired with blatant disbelief. She kept his calendar up to the minute with his appointments and he never, ever, slipped one in without telling her about it. It was an ingrained, orderly habit, and he knew she knew it.

"Somewhere, anywhere," he muttered anyway, disengaging himself from the embrace and grabbing his jacket.

He practically bolted for the door, not daring to look back. Someday he'd have to explain, but not now. Now, if he stayed, explanations would be the last thing on his mind. In fact, he doubted if either of them would be doing any thinking at all. What

they were feeling could keep them occupied—pleas-
antly, dangerously occupied—for days.

And it would be more wrong now than it had ever
been.

## Chapter Ten

Well, that was certainly fascinating, Zelda thought as she absentmindedly rebuttoned her jacket and straightened her skirt. For Taylor to lose control in the office, his feelings had to run a lot deeper than he was willing to admit. If it had been nothing more than lust, he probably would have fired her on the spot just to avoid further temptation.

The fact that he didn't return to the office for the rest of the day didn't particularly surprise her. He always had been one for sorting things out in private. If he considered succumbing to his emotions a weakness, then he'd go to any extreme to avoid having her witness another lapse. Witness? No. Instigate was more like it. She wondered how long he'd manage to stay away and bet herself it would be hours, rather than days.

The challenge of seeing to it that he lapsed quite a bit made her smile. In fact, it cheered her up so much that she bought another can of raspberry paint for the living room walls that she'd stripped of that dreary cabbage rose wallpaper over the weekend.

She had the stereo on full blast and was paint spattered from head to toe, when she sensed that she was no longer alone. In Los Angeles that awareness would have had her tumbling from atop the ladder in a panic. Now she merely glanced over her shoulder and grinned at her expected visitor.

"Hi, Taylor."

Mouth gaping, he was staring not at her, but the walls. "What the hell kind of color is this?"

"Raspberry. Isn't it wonderful?"

"That's not the word I would have chosen."

"Let me guess. Bright? Flamboyant?"

"How about blinding?"

"Wait until I get the new curtains up and re-cover the sofa. With a little white woodwork, it'll be warm and cozy."

"Warm and cozy?" he echoed skeptically. "Couldn't you have picked some subtle, muted shade that's a little easier on the eyes?"

"White, I suppose?"

"White, cream, gray."

She grinned at him. "Boring. By the way, I don't suppose you happened to notice that the outside is the same color."

"No kidding!"

"Nope. Sarah Lynn's reaction was a lot like yours. If this keeps up, I wouldn't be surprised to have the mayor institute a new ordinance restricting the exterior paint on all houses to white after this."

"Not altogether a bad idea," Taylor said with feeling. "Look, have you had dinner? I was thinking maybe we ought to sit down and discuss what happened at work today."

"You mean your father's visit?" she said, being deliberately obtuse.

He scowled at her. "No. I think that pretty well spoke for itself. I meant what happened after that."

"When I tried to seduce you?"

For an instant Taylor looked unnerved, then he laughed. "Ah, Zelda, you never did bother pulling punches, did you?"

She shrugged from her perch on the ladder. It gave her a sense of security sitting above him. Maybe she should insist on holding all conversations with her at this vantage point. "Never saw much point to hedging, especially not with you. You could always read my mind, anyway."

"Maybe then. Not now."

She gave him a slow, lingering perusal, head to toe and back again. "Oh, really?"

He gave a rueful, tolerant shake of his head. "Okay, I know what you're thinking when you do that, but I don't know why."

She didn't take his bewilderment seriously. He knew. He just didn't want to admit it. "The usual reasons, I suppose," she said evasively.

"Which are?"

"Okay, let me spell it out for you. You're sexy. I want your body," she retorted lightly. Then, because he once again looked so thoroughly disconcerted by her directness, her expression sobered. "Some things never change, Taylor." She regarded him evenly. "Do they?"

His gaze locked with hers. For an instant the question appeared to have left him tongue-tied.

"No," he admitted finally and with great reluctance. "I guess they never do."

The admission hovered between them. Awareness hummed through the air. It took every last ounce of willpower Zelda possessed not to launch herself into his arms. But she was wise enough for once to see that Taylor was still struggling with some inner turmoil. She had to give him time to wrestle with it on his own.

At least through dinner.

"You still interested in dinner?" she said eventually. "I fixed some beef stew earlier. I'll share, if you'll help me paint."

"I'm wearing a suit," he said, as if that wasn't already obvious.

The gray pinstripes were quietly tasteful and becoming. That didn't stop her from wanting to strip him down to basics.

"You don't have to be," she taunted for the second time that day.

Taylor shook his head. "You never give up, do you?"

She nodded in agreement. "Not while there's breath in my body."

To her astonishment, Taylor shucked his jacket and shirt, an act that lacked the finesse of a Vegas stripper, but practically had her panting for more. Unfortunately, though, he stopped there.

"You'll ruin those pants," she warned, an undeniably hopeful note in her voice.

"It's an old suit," he retorted, shooting her a knowing look that made her blood heat. "Now give me a brush and let's get this finished. I'm starved."

Zelda was hungry, too, but beef stew was the last thing that appealed to her appetite. Why did it have to be this complex man with a will of iron who tantalized her? she wondered in dismay. There were successful, handsome, intelligent men in Los Angeles. Her boss's new stepfather, who adored meddling, was more than willing to play matchmaker. But no, she had to come back to a town she hated and a man she had every reason to despise to rediscover this jittery, head-over-heels feeling again. Sometimes fate was a damned nuisance.

"Do you think we could turn the stereo down a little?" Taylor asked eventually. "They can probably hear it in the next county."

She regarded him with a defiant tilt to her chin. "So what?"

Taylor opened his mouth, then clamped it shut again, apparently recognizing a challenge no matter how it was phrased. Whatever argument had been on the tip of his tongue, he kept to himself. Zelda winked at him. "That's more like it," she told him approvingly.

Taylor's expression underwent a slow transformation from indignation to something far more dangerous. He gestured to her, a provocative come-hither wave of his fingers. "Come down off that ladder."

Zelda was no slouch when it came to recognizing a dare, either. She shook her head, just to see how far Taylor was willing to go. "Uh-uh," she said piously. "I've got work to do. So do you."

"Now who's being stuffy, Ms. Lane? Remember this song?"

Zelda hadn't really been paying that much attention to which albums were blaring from the stereo. She just liked all that cheerful noise, that throbbing rhythm. Now she listened more closely and recognized a song that she and Taylor had once claimed as their own. It wasn't slow. It wasn't subtle. In fact, the provocative rhythm was as daring as their love had once been.

"Come on, sugar," he taunted with that lazy drawl that snaked along her spine like pure desire. "Let's see if you've still got those moves."

A deliberate challenge could only be resisted for so long. With her gaze locked with Taylor's, Zelda descended from the ladder. He reached for her hand the instant her feet hit the floor and spun her around. His hips swayed seductively. Hers matched the music's beat. His shoulders counterpointed the rhythm. Relaxing into the music, hers mimicked his. The moves were graceful and as natural as if they'd been practicing them every day of their lives. They circled the room, intent on capturing the music's boldly provocative essence.

Zelda could feel the rhythm deep inside her, its tug almost sexual, especially with Taylor's appreciative gaze lingering on the rise and fall of her breasts, the sensual movements of her hips. Without even touching, they turned the dance into something intimate, four minutes of pure heat that teased the senses and invited acts far more exciting.

When the song ended, they faced each other, breathless, exhilarated, and wanting the one thing neither of them dared. Zelda knew that it would take no more than one gesture—a hand extended, a single step—and they would be making love, turning that subtle, smoldering heat into a blazing fire from which there would be no turning back.

"We're playing with fire," Taylor said softly, as if he'd read her mind.

"Is there some reason we shouldn't?" she asked, her own voice husky with unspoken needs.

Taylor sighed. "I can think of dozens."

"Name one."

"I have a daughter."

"Who's not in this room."

"I have nothing to offer. I can't make you pretty promises. It would be just like before. We'd have this *fling,* get our emotions all tangled up, and then I'd end up hurting you."

"Are you so sure of that?" she said, defeated by his apparent certainty.

Taylor nodded, his eyes bleak. "It's what I do best," he said, reaching for his shirt and jacket.

He didn't stop to pull either of them on, just brushed a kiss across Zelda's forehead and walked out, leaving her alone again. And filled with yearning.

Not even that bright pink paint was a match for the depression that settled over her.

"Zelda, it's Caitlin. Remember?"

Zelda recognized not only the name, but the loneliness and wistful cry for attention in the child's tone. "Hi, sweetheart," she said, shifting the phone to her other ear so she could write down a message. "Did you want to talk to your father? He's out of the office right now."

"I wanted to talk to you," Caitlin said. "Did you forget we were going to go shopping?"

Zelda hadn't forgotten, but she had been putting it off. With everything between her and Taylor growing more awkward day by day thanks to the undeniable and powerful reawakening of their hormones, she hadn't wanted to complicate things even further by getting too close to his daughter.

"I've been so busy the last couple of weeks, I haven't been able to get a single minute free. I'm sorry."

"Oh." Caitlin's voice sank dispiritedly. "I guess if you're too busy, I could call Grandmother."

Of all the things Caitlin might have said, she'd managed to pick the one guaranteed to get Zelda's attention. "No," she said hurriedly, imagining another one of those proper little outfits. "A promise is a promise. Tomorrow's Saturday. Would that be a good day?"

"Are you sure there's still time to make a dress before next weekend? That's when my party is."

"That will be plenty of time. I'll call your headmistress as soon as we hang up and make the arrangements for tomorrow. I'll pick you up at nine so we'll have the whole day."

"You don't need to call," Caitlin said. "She's right here. She let me use her phone."

Zelda grinned. "Put her on, then. I'll see you in the morning."

After the arrangements were finalized and Zelda had hung up, she sat back and mentally congratulated Caitlin. Even at seven, she was a kid who knew exactly what she wanted and how to go about getting it. Maybe there was a lesson or two she could learn from the pint-size strategist.

At eight the next morning she grabbed her keys and headed for the door. Before she could reach it, someone knocked. Force of habit made her peek through the curtains to see who it was. Taylor stood on the porch wearing jeans, a blue oxford-cloth shirt open at the throat, and a khaki jacket. Trying to hide her astonishment, she opened the door.

"Good morning. What brings you by?"

"A command performance," he muttered dryly. "Caitlin was afraid you wouldn't find her school."

"I see. Did you explain to her about maps and directions?"

"In detail. Then she cried," he said. "I really hate it when she cries. Unfortunately, she knows it." He regarded Zelda helplessly. "Is that a genetic thing with females? Do you all just know automatically how to get your way with men?"

Zelda laughed at his genuine bewilderment. "Taylor, if that were true, I'd have landed you long ago." She hesitated thoughtfully. "Of course, I haven't considered tears."

"Don't," he pleaded. "Are you ready?"

"Oh, I'm ready," she said, reminding herself to buy Caitlin the fanciest material she could find, along with a double hot-fudge sundae. She owed her a lot more than that just for this first lesson alone.

Mostly hidden in a grove of ancient oaks, Caitlin's school sat high atop a hill overlooking a wide sweep of lawn that ended at the river's edge. Only a discreet sign at the front gate identified it as being a school rather than someone's home. Spanish moss hung from the live oaks that lined the winding driveway.

When they reached the circular drive in front of the main entrance Zelda had a clearer view of the school itself. Constructed of gray fieldstone, the building's additions looked as if they'd been haphazardly tacked on to make room for an ever-increasing student population. To Zelda it seemed reminiscent of pictures she'd seen of some British country school.

As if she'd been watching from the windows, Caitlin ran out to greet them. Before either her father or Zelda could step out of the car, Caitlin had flung herself into the back seat.

"Hi, Daddy. I missed you," she said, hugging him around the neck from behind.

"Apparently so," he said dryly. "I thought you and Zelda had planned to make this a girl's outing."

"It'll be more fun with you, though," Caitlin said. "Won't it, Zelda?"

Zelda glanced over her shoulder and winked. "Definitely more fun."

"Besides, Zelda doesn't know where the best malls are," Caitlin rationalized.

"And you do?" Taylor said.

"No, Daddy, that's why we need you."

"Oh. I thought I was just along to carry the shopping bags."

"That, too," Zelda said. "It's always good to have a big, strong man along to do the heavy labor, right, Caitlin?"

"Right."

He glanced up into the rearview mirror and regarded his daughter with mock ferocity. "You used to be such a sweet little girl."

"I'm still sweet, but I'm not a little girl," Caitlin replied indignantly. "I'm almost eight. And I want a grown-up dress, not some baby thing with ruffles. Okay?"

"I'll leave that in Zelda's capable hands," he said. He glanced over and studied the vintage dress she'd chosen to wear for the outing. "On the other hand, perhaps I should have let you crawl around in your grandmother's attic. She has lots of trunks up there filled with old dresses just like the one Zelda is wearing."

Caitlin scrambled up until she could peer over the back of the seat. "I think Zelda's dress is beautiful."

"Thank you. Your father obviously has a very traditional sense of fashion. Naturally for an occasion as important as your birthday, we want something original, something with a little flair."

"Something that will give my mother palpitations?" he suggested dryly.

Zelda grinned at him. "If at all possible."

He groaned. "How did I know that?"

In the end they compromised over a pattern for a dress that was both elegant and simple. Caitlin regarded the style with disdain until Zelda led her to the bolts of fabric and found the perfect shade of teal blue velvet. Caitlin touched it carefully, her eyes growing round.

"Oh, my," she whispered. "It's so soft. It's the same color as those ducks we saw last winter, isn't it, Daddy?"

"Exactly the same color." Taylor's expression turned gentle. "You will look beautiful in it," he promised. His gaze caught Zelda's. "So would you."

"Oh, yes," Caitlin said at once. "Make one for you just like mine."

A charming image of mother-daughter outfits flashed briefly in Zelda's mind, then she shook her head. She had no right. "I don't need a new dress. Besides, this material is outrageously expensive."

"My treat," Taylor said. "A thank-you gift for making Caitlin so happy."

Zelda fingered the material longingly. It was truly magnificent. "Maybe just enough for a skirt," she agreed finally, already envisioning the slender lines of it with a daring slit up the back.

When the purchase had been made, Caitlin led them to the mall's food court. "Ice cream," she announced.

"A balanced lunch, then ice cream," Taylor countered.

Zelda rolled her eyes. "Come on. This is a rare treat. There are no rules."

Taylor looked as if he weren't quite sure what to do without a set of dietary guidelines. He glanced around at the various options.

"Okay," he said finally, "you two go for broke. I think I'll have a grilled chicken sandwich."

Zelda planted herself in front of him. "Do you really want a grilled chicken sandwich or is that the only healthy thing you could identify?"

"Healthy habit," he admitted.

"Okay, now, close your eyes," she insisted. "Let all those decadent food choices flow through your mind. Think of this as a day at a carnival or a celebration. What would you really, really like if you couldn't hear your mother or your doctor whispering in your ear?"

He closed his eyes, apparently taking the game she'd suggested seriously. "Nachos," he confessed slowly. "A big plate of chips, covered with cheese and refried beans and sour cream and salsa."

"That's it," Zelda told him approvingly. "Now you sit right over there and I will bring that to you."

Taylor laughed. "You really don't need to wait on me. I can get it myself."

"But you won't. You'll have an attack of conscience halfway over there and come back with that grilled chicken sandwich. Worse, you'll find some-place that makes a salad and has diet dressing.''

"You know me too well," he said, still laughing, looking more carefree than he had since the day she came back into town. "Maybe you're good for me, after all."

The surprising admission, made thoughtfully and with some obvious reluctance, was still enough to make Zelda's heart sing.

Minutes later she and Caitlin returned with trays laden with nachos, pizza and ice cream. Taylor groaned. "We'll all wind up with clogged arteries."

"Not from one day's indulgence," Zelda insisted. "Now don't spoil this. Just enjoy."

His gaze met hers as she bit into the cheesy pizza. With her tongue she tried to catch a strand of errant mozzarella. His eyes deliberately followed every movement, locking onto her tongue in a way that made her pulse buck and made her forget all about food. Her imagination kicked in. She could have been eating sawdust.

Suddenly all she could think about was the rough texture of Taylor's skin, the salty taste of it against her tongue, the way it heated beneath her touch. When he brushed a finger across her lips to wipe away a dab of tomato sauce, she swallowed hard. When he slowly, deliberately, licked the sauce from his finger, she felt the tug of pure longing all the way to her toes. Dear heaven, it was like making love in public.

Dazed, she glanced around guiltily, her gaze finally settling on Caitlin, who was clearly so absorbed with her huge sundae that she was oblivious to whatever was going on between her father and Zelda. When she finally dared another look at Taylor, he, too, seemed innocently unaware of the havoc he had wreaked with her senses. He was busily piling a chip high with cheese and salsa.

Finally, just as he was about to put it into his mouth, he grinned at her. "Nothing like a little spice to liven things up, huh?"

Zelda figured if Taylor Matthews brought much more spice into her life without following through, she'd be limp as a dishrag.

## Chapter Eleven

As the day wore on and Caitlin grew tired and cranky from too much excitement, Taylor watched in wonder as Zelda easily teased a smile back onto her face. From the instant they had met, it had been evident that the two were soulmates. He envied them that easy camaraderie.

In most ways Zelda's easy rapport with his daughter delighted him. That didn't stop him from worrying about what would happen when Zelda left Port William. He determinedly pushed the worry aside because by the end of their shopping expedition, Taylor saw a glimmer of the exuberant, lively child he'd dropped off at boarding school for the first time back in September. He would be eternally grateful that his child's natural liveliness had been restored.

Another thought kept sneaking in as he watched the pair of them, one he couldn't readily dismiss. He wondered if he'd misjudged Zelda all these years. She seemed to know instinctively all the things about parenting that bemused him. She was gentle and patient. She listened. Caitlin was visibly blossoming under all the attention. How could someone who lived selfishly and thoroughly in the moment without a thought for anything beyond that be so attuned to a child's needs? Unless, of course, there was more substance there than he'd been giving her credit for. Of course, it wouldn't be the first time in his life he'd been blind to the truth.

Whatever that truth was in this instance, he was pleased for Caitlin. He couldn't—he wouldn't—take this friendship away from her unnecessarily. She'd already lost too much in her young life.

But just how was he supposed to protect himself from the warmth that spread through him just being around the two of them? Zelda's teasing always included him. Her eyes sparkled like rare gems whenever she looked his way. And her laughter, which she shared unstintingly, eased an ache deep inside him.

As they left the mall, he found himself instinctively reaching for her hand, folding it in his own, marveling at how right it felt, even as the reaction scared the daylights out of him. He had vowed never again to be taken in by a woman's wiles, yet here he was, mesmerized. He had vowed always to let his head overrule his emotions, yet here he was, lost to sensation.

They drove back to Graystone School with the exhausted Caitlin wedged between them. Her head drooped, then came to rest on Zelda's shoulder. He watched a little enviously as she smoothed his daughter's hair from her cheeks, her fingers caressing the soft skin with evident wonder written on her face.

As if she sensed his gaze on her, she glanced over at him.

"You're so lucky, Taylor," she whispered with an unmistakable catch in her voice. Tears shimmered in her eyes. "It must be so wonderful to watch a child grow, to nurture her and know that a part of you will live on in her."

"I suppose," he said, wishing that he could feel the joy as readily as he could the fear. Though he couldn't say it aloud, certainly not with Caitlin nearby and merely drowsing, he was terrified to think that it was not just his genes in his daughter, but Maribeth's. What if her careless nature was what Caitlin had inherited? What if his daughter lived too short a life because she, too, thrived on danger?

And what, he finally asked himself, what if Zelda was ultimately destroyed because of the same addiction to reckless acts? He wasn't sure he could bear another such loss. Wasn't that the bottom line that explained his holding back when he wanted nothing more than to have her back in his bed and in his life?

Zelda regarded him intently, as if she could sense his unspoken reservations without possibly being able to guess the cause. "Taylor?" she said questioningly.

He shook his head, mustering a faint grin. "Don't mind me. Sometimes I get so caught up in what-ifs, I forget to live in the here and now."

"I don't understand."

"There's no reason you should," he said. To avoid further explanation, he directed his full attention to the road ahead. When they arrived at Graystone, he carried Caitlin inside, hoping that by the time he got back to the car, Zelda would have forgotten all about his enigmatic remarks.

Naturally, though, she hadn't. The minute he got behind the wheel, she regarded him evenly. "Suppose you tell me whatever it was you were trying so hard not to say a few minutes ago."

"I don't know what you mean."

"Damn it, Taylor, ever since I got back to town you and everybody else have been hinting that there's some deep, dark secret about your marriage. Now I get the feeling that it has something to do with your daughter, maybe even explains why you've shipped her off to boarding school when a kid her age needs to be at home where she's loved."

A protective anger, already simmering just below the surface, boiled over. "Don't you dare criticize the way I've chosen to raise my daughter," he snapped, wondering if she realized she was starting an argument he'd already had a dozen times with his parents and himself. "You don't know anything about it."

"I know that she's lost and lonely. I know that she adores you and that she doesn't understand why you don't love her."

He simply stared at her, shocked and angered by the unfair accusation. "How can you say I don't love her?" he retorted in a low, amazingly even voice. A deadly calm stole over him, the calm that preceded a storm, he knew from experience.

Zelda laid a hand on his arm. "I'm not saying it. I'm saying it's what Caitlin thinks."

The explanation did nothing to soothe his desire to lash out. "You've seen her twice. What makes you think you know anything at all about what she thinks?"

"Because when I look into her eyes, I see myself at that age," she said, her voice suddenly flat and emotionless, her eyes haunted. "I see the same questions, the same longing, the same hurt. I know what it's like to have one parent you want more than anything to please, a parent who'll never think you're good enough. I know what it's like to have another parent who loves you, but who is distant and withdrawn, a laughingstock."

She lifted her gaze to his. A lone tear spilled down her cheek and something inside him wrenched at the sight.

"It hurts, Taylor," she whispered. "Even now, years later, just thinking about the loneliness in that house makes my heart ache. Caitlin deserves better than that."

His anger disintegrated at once. With fingers that trembled, he brushed away the tear. "Oh, sugar, that was a long time ago. You survived. You turned out just fine."

"Did I? Then why did I run away? Why did I spend ten years hiding out in Los Angeles, where I wouldn't have to deal with any of the pain? Why couldn't I even come back for my own mother's funeral?"

"You're here now. I think she knew you'd come."

"Eventually," she replied bitterly. "She saw to that."

"Maybe because she always knew how badly you needed to come home and find peace."

Zelda's gaze shot to his and the hopeful glint in her eyes nearly staggered him.

"Do you think that was why she wrote the will the way she did?" she demanded. "Do you think she understood me better than I realized?"

"You're here, aren't you? Are you at peace with the memories?"

Zelda seemed to consider the question thoughtfully, before slowly nodding. "Yes," she said finally, a smile breaking through. "You know, I really am. Sometime in the past weeks I've accepted the fact that my father was who he was. My mother and I could have turned cartwheels and it wouldn't have changed anything. I'm sad for her, sad that he destroyed her life, but I don't hate him for it anymore. And I won't allow him to continue affecting my choices from beyond the grave."

"So coming back hasn't been all bad, has it?" he said.

An impish gleam suddenly sparked in her eyes, putting Taylor immediately on alert.

"Definitely not all bad. Of course," she said slyly, "I think she had another motive in mind all along, too."

Taylor responded to that spark of mischief. "Oh, and what was that?"

She opened her mouth to reply, then shook her head. "Nope. I think I'll keep that one to myself, at least until I see how it turns out." Her gaze narrowed. "You've managed to get me off track, Taylor Matthews, but now it's your turn. Just what is it about having Caitlin at home that worries you so?"

"I can't spend enough time with her," he evaded.

"She's in school all day. Your office is part of the house, so it won't be like she's coming home to an empty place. If that's really a problem, you could afford to hire a housekeeper."

"She needs discipline."

The statement was greeted with obvious puzzlement. "She's the most well-behaved child I know."

Taylor lost patience. "Look, it's just not a good idea, okay. Drop it."

His sharp tone silenced her for the rest of the ride back to Port William. But Taylor knew Zelda well enough by now to realize that the discussion was far from over.

The following Saturday Zelda was halfway out on a branch of an oak tree, with Caitlin scrambling along just ahead of her, when she heard Taylor's cry of panic. Or was it outrage? She couldn't quite tell from her perch high above the ground. A glance down into stormy gray eyes solved it. He was furious.

"What's wrong?" she called down.

"Have you lost your mind?" he muttered indignantly, hovering beneath them as if he were just waiting for one of them to drop into his arms.

Zelda had a feeling if she were the one crashing down, he just might let her go. "Come on up," she suggested. "You used to be able to beat me to the top."

"I was younger then and didn't have a lick of sense." He groaned. "Caitlin, honey, come on down."

Caitlin's chin rose mutinously. "No. You can see everywhere from up here. Zelda says you did this all the time when you were my age."

"I was a boy. Boys climbed trees. Little girls..."

"Zelda climbed, too."

"That doesn't make it right," he snapped.

Zelda could see that the adventure she'd promised Caitlin wasn't working out quite the way they'd planned it. If she didn't get her safely out of this tree this instant, Taylor was going to ruin her birthday by confining her to her room.

"We'll be right down," she promised. "Just let me show her where you carved our initials in the trunk."

"Carved our initials?" Taylor repeated weakly. "Zelda, how do you even know this is the same tree?"

"I wouldn't forget something like that," she retorted indignantly. She reached up and felt along the bark until she came to the ragged heart. She grinned triumphantly. "See, they're right here."

"I want to see," Caitlin insisted, inching past Zelda. She pulled herself upright and lovingly traced the initials inside the heart. "How old were you when you did this, Daddy?"

"Older than you. Now get down from there. And be careful."

"Oh, Daddy," Caitlin muttered with obvious disgust. With an obviously inherited agility and intrepid spirit, she scampered down.

"Into the house," Taylor ordered. "We'll discuss this in a minute."

Undaunted, Caitlin grinned up at Zelda. "See you."

"See you," Zelda echoed.

"Come on down," Taylor said when his daughter was out of sight. "Face the music."

Zelda shook her head and leaned back against the tree trunk. "I don't think so. The view from up here is terrific."

A smile tugged at Taylor's lips, ruining his scowl. "It's not bad from down here," he taunted, gazing up toward her bottom. "Zelda, you just scared ten years off of my life."

"Why?" she asked, genuinely confused.

"I don't think Caitlin's ever been up in a tree before."

"Then it was past time she tried it."

"She could have fallen and broken her neck."

"And she could break a leg going down the stairs at school," Zelda replied reasonably.

"Not if she's careful."

"Have you ever seen an eight-year-old be careful on the stairs or anywhere else? Taylor, you can't protect her from everything."

"But I can keep the odds in her favor."

"By keeping her out of trees?"

"Yes, damn it. I won't have her taking risks. Now will you please get down from there? I'm getting a crick in my neck trying to talk to you."

"Then come on up."

"Zelda!"

"You want to talk, I'm available, but I'm not budging."

"You are the most stubborn—" he grumbled as he grabbed onto the tree's lowest branch and hauled himself up "—most impossible woman it has ever been my misfortune to know."

"But who else could get you to climb a tree?" she countered.

"Not many would even want me to."

"Boring, the whole lot of them."

"There's a lot to be said for boring," he told her, his tone far more serious than the teasing conversation warranted.

"Not much that I can think of," she retorted, watching his face closely in an attempt to judge his reaction.

"Zelda, people get killed taking risks," he said, his tone angry.

"Some of them do," she said slowly, beginning to get an idea of what was behind all the changes she'd seen in him since her return. Her voice dropped a level. "Was Maribeth one of them?"

His expression bleak, he avoided her gaze. "Yes," he admitted eventually. "She drove like a maniac, all the time, even when she was drunk. Which," he added, "was more often than not."

"So she died taking a stupid, unnecessary risk," Zelda whispered, reaching for Taylor's hand. "You can't blame yourself for that. And you can't assume that the rest of us will be so careless."

"But you are. You always have been. And Caitlin is showing all the signs of being the same way."

Zelda felt as if she'd been punched in the stomach. "That's why you sent her away, isn't it? That's why you're so worried about her being disciplined?"

He nodded. "I couldn't bear it if anything happened to her."

Zelda raised his hand to her lips and kissed his knuckles, knuckles scarred by a dozen childish misadventures, most of them involving her. She understood him now, understood the anguish that guided him. What she didn't know, couldn't even begin to fathom, was how to prove to him that life never, ever, came with guarantees, no matter how careful a person was to follow all the rules.

Zelda had had no idea that ten eight-year-old girls could make so much noise. Otherwise she might not have encouraged Taylor to give them the run of the house.

"How much mischief can they possibly get into?" she'd said only minutes before every single door upstairs had slammed shut in succession. The crashes had been interspersed with the thundering of little patent-leather-shoed feet.

"What are they doing?" Taylor inquired, regarding her as if any disasters were all her fault.

"Playing, most likely."

"Playing what? War?"

That would have been Zelda's guess, but she wasn't about to admit it. "Wine?" she suggested. "It'll relax you."

Taylor shook his head. "Something tells me I need to be fully alert for whatever's about to come our way."

"Think of it this way. Caitlin is having a birthday party she'll never forget."

"That makes two of us," he muttered with heartfelt conviction.

"There, there," she consoled. "Let's get the cake and ice cream ready. At least that will get them down here where we can keep an eye on them."

"Good idea. I'll scoop. You carry. When it's on the table, yell upstairs and then stand back out of the way."

Not twenty minutes later, ten girls were sitting demurely at the dining-room table. Zelda tried not to notice that the sleeve of one child's dress was ripped, or that another's hair bow was slipping dangerously. She even managed to ignore the fact that half of them were no longer wearing shoes or socks. It was more difficult to pretend not to see that all of them had on more eye makeup than a Hollywood Boulevard hooker. Taylor stared at them, clearly dazed.

He latched onto her arm and dragged her into the kitchen. "What am I supposed to tell their parents?"

"Some of them are staying here. We'll have time to clean them up. As for the rest, leave any telling to them. They'll be so busy talking about what a wonderful time they had, maybe their parents won't even notice the rest."

Taylor regarded her skeptically. "I think you're being overly optimistic."

As if to provide backup for his claim, the front door opened and Geraldine and Beau Matthews swept in. Zelda's heart sank. There was no chance *they* wouldn't notice that things had gotten just ever-so-slightly out of control.

Ignoring Zelda, they headed straight for the dining room and practically skidded to a horrified stop.

"Grandma," Caitlin squealed, bouncing down from her chair and running to throw her arms around her grandmother's waist. To Geraldine Matthews's credit, she managed to cover her dismay at the prospect of having pink blusher and peach lipstick smeared down the front of her dress.

"Hi, darling. Happy birthday! Are you having a good time?"

Caitlin looked up, displaying mascaraed lashes and a significant amount of Zelda's blue eye shadow. "The best time I've ever had. Thanks for the cake. I ate three roses. We've got ice cream, too."

"Strawberry and chocolate, I'll bet," her grandmother said.

It was an easy guess, given the streaks down the front of Caitlin's beautiful velvet dress.

"Do you and Granddaddy want some?" Caitlin asked.

"Maybe later. You can save us a piece. We just wanted to stop by with your present."

Caitlin looked from one to the other with obvious puzzlement. Zelda shared her confusion. Neither grandparent was carrying a thing.

"Outside," Beau said, as if he'd just then recovered the power of speech and was afraid to waste words.

Caitlin's eyes widened. "You got me a pony, didn't you?" she said, bouncing excitedly. "I thought you forgot."

"We'd never forget our promises to you, pumpkin," Beau said, shooting a warning look in Taylor's direction. "The filly's a beauty, if I do say so myself."

As Caitlin ran outside with her grandparents, her friends raced after them, leaving cake and melting ice cream behind. Zelda kept her eyes on Taylor. There was no mistaking the anguish written on his face, or the barely controlled fury.

"You didn't want her to have a pony, did you?"

"No, and they knew that. We discussed it again just last week."

"But she's so happy," Zelda pointed out.

"Well, of course, she is," he retorted impatiently. "What little girl wouldn't be ecstatic to have her own horse? That's not the issue."

"What is?"

"She's not old enough to ride. She could get hurt. And they knew exactly how strongly I felt about that," he said, striding toward the door.

His intentions were all too clear. Zelda stepped into his path. "Please," she said. "Don't spoil this for her. Or for them, for that matter. They just did it to please her, not to defy you."

"I'm not so sure about that," he said dryly. "What am I supposed to do? Go against everything I feel as a concerned parent just to keep the peace?"

"For this one day," she said. "Let Caitlin be thrilled. There will be time enough tomorrow to set all the rules and regulations you want to about when she can ride and how much supervision she has to have."

"What about just taking the damned horse back?"

"Is that really what you want to do? Or do you just want to make sure that she acts responsibly?"

He finally sighed heavily. "I just want to keep my child safe."

Zelda wound her arms around his waist and kissed the deep furrow in his brow. "There's more than one way to do that, Taylor. Caution is not the same as denial."

He went absolutely still as he pondered what she'd said. Zelda could feel his heartbeat, steady and sure.

"Has anyone ever told you that you're a very wise woman?" he said finally.

"Not in this town."

A hint of amusement sparked in his eyes, along with something else. "I can think of some other activities to which that caution-denial adage might apply."

Zelda's pulse skipped a beat. "And what might those be?"

"Stick around after we get rid of these little hellions and I just might show you."

## Chapter Twelve

An entire night with four little girls in the house and Zelda down the hall in the guest room tested Taylor's willpower, to say nothing of his hearing and his patience.

"They never slept," he grumbled to Zelda over coffee at 7:00 a.m. "Not for one single minute."

"How do you know that?" she asked, yawning herself, but trying to hide it from him.

Suddenly he realized this was the first time he and Zelda had spent an entire night under the same roof. That set off a whole new round of fascinating speculation.

He decided he liked sitting across a breakfast table from her when she was still a little mussed, her face free of makeup, her clothes tugged on haphazardly—jeans and a T-shirt and not much else as near as he could tell. Her feet, propped on another chair, were bare, her toenails painted a shocking red.

With a sense of resignation, he realized that all he could think about anymore was stripping away the clothes, taking her back to bed and making love to her all morning long. Slow, leisurely love-making. His body responded just thinking about it.

"Taylor!"

He blinked. "Sorry. What?"

"I asked how you knew the girls were up all night."

"Because they kept me awake."

She sipped her coffee and regarded him skeptically over the rim of the cup. "*They* kept you awake," she repeated, casting a knowing look at him.

"Well, of course," he grumbled, refusing to admit that it was Zelda's presence—so near, yet so unattainable—that had kept him tossing and turning. His vehement comment didn't seem to fool her, though. Amusement was dancing in her eyes.

"Don't mess with me," he warned.

"I wouldn't dream of it," she said innocently. "Not while there are children in the house."

"That is not what I meant."

"Oh?" she said with that smug expression back on her face.

"I suppose you slept all night."

"Like a baby."

"Humph!"

"Of course, it did occur to me once or twice that I would have been getting a lot less sleep if I'd been a couple of rooms down the hall."

A satisfied smile spread across his face. "So, the truth comes out at last."

"Yeah, those kids sounded as if they were having a wonderful time."

Taylor groaned. "Very funny."

"What's on the agenda for today?"

"I don't suppose I could convince them all we should take naps until, say, midafternoon?"

"Not likely. My guess is that they're all going to want to go over to your parents' house so they can ride Daisy. I'm surprised Caitlin didn't beg to take the horse upstairs with her last night, just so she could remind herself she was real."

"Actually she tried for keeping her in the backyard. I said no." Taylor drained the rest of the coffee and wished desperately that he had some aspirin nearby. Just thinking about that horse made his blood run cold and his head pound.

"But you will take her out there today," Zelda prodded.

"Not a chance in hell," he said flatly. "And first thing tomorrow I am going to have a talk with my father. If he wants to keep the horse, that's up to him, but I won't have Caitlin over there risking her neck."

"Now, Taylor," she said quietly, "you can't disappoint Caitlin and her friends."

"Why is that? Who's in charge around here, anyway?"

"You are," she said dutifully.

He could tell at once she didn't mean it.

"And I know you love Caitlin and only want what's best for her, just as your father always wanted what was best for you."

"Low blow," he muttered, glaring at her.

She watched him expectantly, just waiting to see if she'd scored a direct hit, no doubt. She had.

"Maybe it would be okay if we went over so they could feed the horse," he conceded finally.

"Maybe ride her around the paddock with you leading the horse?" she suggested.

He threw up his hands in a gesture of resignation. "Okay, okay. Damn it, you're worse than Caitlin."

She shook her head. "I'm just trying to save you from all those tears."

He regarded her malevolently. "Right. I'm going to take a shower."

"Good. A nice, cold, reviving one, I hope. You'll definitely need all your wits about you to get through the rest of the day."

"You know, you could be replaced," he muttered as he left the kitchen.

"I dare you to try," she called after him, her tone too blasted cheerful.

"Don't tempt me," he shot back, determined, just this once, to have the last word.

The horse seemed awfully big. Though Beau assured him the filly was gentle as a lamb, Taylor was absolutely certain there was a mean glint in the animal's eyes. He glared over at Zelda for talking him into this peace-making trip out to his parents' house.

It was too late now to back out, though. With Zelda instructing them, four little girls were holding out their hands, palms flat, a chunk of carrot in the center. Taylor was certain the horse was going to chomp down on more than the carrot at any second. He observed with his heart in his throat.

"Can we ride her?" Caitlin said, approaching him, her expression pleading. "Please, Daddy?"

"Well, of course you can, sweet pea," Beau said before Taylor could open his mouth. "Why else would I buy you a horse, if I didn't intend to teach you to ride?"

Taylor gritted his teeth. "Once around the paddock," he said reluctantly. "Granddaddy will walk you."

"All of us?" Caitlin asked.

"You can take turns," Taylor agreed.

Zelda, who'd kept her distance from his father and mostly from Taylor, walked over to stand beside him as his father boosted Caitlin into the saddle. The intrepid child never even glanced down at the ground. He supposed her total lack of fear should please him, but it did just the opposite. It was just more evidence that Caitlin was going to have to be watched like a hawk if she was going to grow up in one piece.

"Relax," Zelda whispered, sliding her hand along his spine until it came to rest at the small of his back, right at the edge of his belt.

If she'd meant to distract him, he had to admit she was doing a pretty decent job of it. Even with his gaze riveted on his daughter, his body was completely aware of the woman at his side.

"You're pressing your luck, sugar," he warned lightly, his gaze never wavering from Caitlin who'd reached the far side of the paddock. She looked over and waved at him, her expression filled with excitement. Taylor managed a tight smile and an unenthusiastic wave.

Zelda's hand crept even lower, though her own gaze was directed toward Caitlin, as well. She was finally relinquishing Daisy to one of her friends. He breathed a sigh of relief, even though he knew the morning was long from over.

"One more inch and you are going to be in a heap of trouble," he advised, suddenly feeling more cheerful.

"What kind of trouble?" she inquired in a tone that was all innocent curiosity. Her expression was pure mischief.

Taylor began to wonder if he was going to get more cooperation than he'd bargained for, after all. How would he cope with a willing Zelda, especially when he wasn't so sure any longer that his intentions, like hers, were only to tease?

"Why don't we go for a stroll and I'll show you?" he suggested anyway, seizing her hand and pulling her in the direction of the old barn that hadn't been used as far back as Taylor could remember. Now, in honor of Caitlin's horse, it had a new coat of paint and, with any luck, a freshly stocked hayloft.

Suddenly Zelda looked just a trifle uncertain, just as he'd anticipated she would. He was almost disappointed. He couldn't resist taunting her a little more. He was playing with fire and he knew it, but it suddenly seemed like an impossible-to-resist game.

"What's the matter?" he inquired. "You're not turning cautious on me, are you?"

She shot a worried look in Beau's direction. "Your parents..."

"My mother's still at church. My father has four little girls to walk around that paddock, several more times if that glint of determination in Caitlin's eyes is any indication."

"I thought you were worried about that."

He shrugged. "You told me everything would be just fine. I've decided to believe you."

Zelda's gaze narrowed suspiciously. "Taylor, what are you up to?"

"Me? You're the one with the roving hands."

"True, but I was just...you know..."

"Trying to distract me?"

"Exactly."

"It worked," he said softly. His gaze lingered on her lips, then slowly drifted down. "It worked very, very well, in fact. Now, come along. You were once rather fond of haylofts, as I recall."

"I was eighteen at the time," she reminded him dryly. "And we got caught."

He winked at her. "And that was the best part, wasn't it?"

She seemed to struggle a bit with her conscience over that one. "Well, yes," she admitted finally.

"Then what's the problem?"

"Old man Highsmith used that shotgun to warn us. Beau'd probably aim it straight at my backside."

"So you're scared," he taunted.

"Not scared," she denied. "Just prudent."

"A fine distinction."

"But an important one." She glanced up at him. "Of course, if you were willing to make it worth my while..."

Taylor's mouth gaped. "You want me to pay you?"

"Not exactly. I want you to take me riding."

"Riding?"

"On Caitlin's horse."

"I'd have to get it away from her first."

"Last I looked, the kids were all heading to the pool. By the way, have I mentioned that I think an indoor pool is totally decadent?"

"No, you hadn't mentioned that," Taylor said, still bemused by her unexpected determination to go horseback riding. She seemed to have developed the obsession rather suddenly. Obviously she was better at this game of bait-and-switch than he was.

"How come you never told me about it before? You don't suppose we could sneak in here some night and go skinny-dipping in that pool?"

He regarded her incredulously as laughter bubbled up. "And you think making it in the barn would be risky? Skinny-dipping in my parents' pool would be suicide. That's why I never told you about it."

She winked at him. "Sounds like fun, though, doesn't it?"

Taylor would not admit that it did, not if he was held down and tortured. Okay, so it wouldn't be the first time they'd done it, but they'd been kids then. Respected attorneys did not sneak around skinny-dipping anywhere, much less where they were almost guaranteed of getting caught. An image of Zelda, all slick with water and bare from head to toe, slammed into his head. That image tested his resolve something fierce.

"I think where we both belong this morning is church, confessing like crazy," he muttered.

"Taylor, we are not Catholic," Zelda reminded him. "And so far, I'd like to point out, we haven't committed any sins. Not lately, anyway."

"That's what you think," he retorted. "Let's go ride the damned horse before I agree to do something really insane.'' He wasn't sure, but he thought he saw Zelda smirk just a little as he turned away. It was all he could do to keep from laughing with sheer exhilaration. She had managed to turn the tables on him once again.

They found the new filly still in the paddock, carefully brushed, her tack removed and placed nearby.

''That's exactly what I was talking about,'' Zelda said. ''Your father has already given them a lesson in responsibility. If they want to ride, then they also have to care for the horse.''

''You've made your point,'' he commented dryly. ''Don't beat it to death.''

''Yes, boss.''

''You only say that when you're trying to irritate me.''

''Works, too, doesn't it?''

Chuckling despite himself, Taylor saddled the horse and swung himself up into the saddle. Zelda stepped on a fence rail, then mounted behind him.

''Once around the paddock?'' he suggested.

''You have to be kidding. Down to the river.''

Her arms circled his waist and she leaned against his back. The soft press of her breasts almost gave him a heart attack. ''Comfortable?'' he inquired dryly.

''Very.''

He set off at a sedate pace. After a few minutes, even with Zelda nestled provocatively against him, he began to relax and enjoy the cool, sunny morning. He filled his lungs with pine-scented air and realized how much he'd missed spending time outdoors. He hadn't even been on a golf course in months, and this part of South Carolina was filled with championship-caliber greens.

"Taylor?"

"Mmm."

"I feel like I'm taking a pony ride at a carnival," she said with an unmistakable sniff of derision.

"Meaning, I suppose, that you'd like to go a little faster."

"If you wouldn't mind. I want to feel the wind rushing through my hair."

"You're wearing one of my old baseball caps," he pointed out.

She punched him playfully in the ribs. "Do you have to take everything so literally?"

"I'm a lawyer. That's what we do."

"Just for today, couldn't you be a wild adventurer? Maybe even a cowboy chasing a cattle rustler?"

"Sugar, I have an active imagination, but I doubt it stretches that far. You create the scenario. I'll pick up the pace."

He nudged the horse into a trot, then a gallop. He had to admit it was more exhilarating.

"Better," Zelda shouted, her voice almost lost in the wind.

Taylor suddenly realized that he felt more alive than he had in years. He was probably going to be sore as the dickens tomorrow and he had a long day in court, but it was worth it to hear Zelda's laughter, to feel this rush of pure adrenaline.

They crested the top of a hill, and the river lay spread below them, its banks blanketed with colorful leaves and pine needles. The setting was peaceful and serene and private.

Taylor was all too aware that Zelda's hands were no longer on his waist, but had drifted to rest on his thighs. His muscles tightened in response. His pulse quickened. He felt as if he'd been aroused for days, as if the need to make love to Zelda had finally overcome every ounce of logic, every reservation. All that verbal teasing had obviously planted some very dangerous notions in his head. And elsewhere.

"Stop," Zelda pleaded now, her voice faintly breathless. Her touch grew bolder, more daring, inflaming his need for her. Caution was looking less and less attractive.

"Not a good idea," Taylor said dutifully, though he did slow the horse to a leisurely pace and tried not to gasp as deft fingers slid over him.

"Actually, it was your idea," she reminded him. "First, last night. Then just a few minutes ago back at the barn."

"Timing is everything. The kids were still there last night. I figured we were safe. You turned me down at the barn, just like I knew you would."

"I've changed my mind," she said, her breath fanning his neck.

Suddenly he felt the touch of her tongue and almost bolted from the saddle. "Zelda, you're not playing fair."

"Nope," she agreed, scattering little kisses over whatever bare flesh she could get to.

Taylor went absolutely still and tried to will himself not to respond. He wanted her so badly right this second he was afraid he'd explode. Wanting her so desperately sent doubts ricocheting through him. He'd vowed never to want anything or anyone this much again.

It would be one thing for them to share a quick roll in the hay, literally or figuratively. It would be quite another to make love, to linger and savor, to touch with joyous abandon, to open up his heart. He was more afraid of that than he ever had been of anything, and that was exactly what would happen if he and Zelda left this horse and allowed their instincts to take over. He would lose control. He would risk yet another loss, more anguish.

He shifted slightly in the saddle and gazed back at her, saw the bright anticipation shining in her eyes, the undeniable yearning that matched his own. Slowly he shook his head. "I can't."

"Can't, or won't?"

"It doesn't really matter, does it? It's too big a risk."

He saw the light in her eyes dim, the proud jut of her chin. "I won't pressure you again," she said stoically.

Her refusal to argue surprised him, maybe even disappointed him. But he could hardly blame her. How many rejections could she be expected to tolerate and still bounce back?

"I think we'd better be getting back," she said, while he struggled with cold honor versus hot need.

Honor, which suddenly tasted an awful lot like fear, won. He turned Daisy around and headed home, aching in more ways than one.

"Zelda?" he said eventually.

"What?" she said impatiently.

"I'm sorry."

She shrugged. "It was a calculated risk. I lost."

No, Taylor thought to himself. He was the one who had lost. He had lost her for the second time in his life. Pain cut through him like a knife.

He urged Daisy into a trot. Then suddenly, to his astonishment, he felt Zelda knee the horse, sending the filly into an all-out gallop. His hands tightened instinctively on the reins, exactly the wrong thing to do. Terrified and confused, the horse bolted on a dangerous course through the woods.

When she raced head-on for a low branch, Taylor saw it in time and ducked, shouting a warning at Zelda in the same instant. Too late! He heard the sickening *thwack* of the limb hitting her, felt her arms slacken around his waist, and then she was sliding. He tried to cling to her, but realized it was no use. Turning as best he could in the saddle, he hooked an arm around her waist, freed his feet from the stirrups and tumbled to the ground, trying desperately to protect Zelda as they landed.

The fall sent a sharp pain shooting down his leg. His butt was likely to be black and blue, but it was Zelda who concerned him. Her eyes were closed. A huge lump was already forming on her forehead. He pressed his finger to the pulse in her neck and was somewhat reassured when he found it strong and steady.

He stroked her forehead, avoiding that nasty lump. "Come on, sugar, wake up," he murmured. With his heart hammering with anxiety, he touched his lips to hers, then gave a rueful smile. Did he think he was Prince Charming and this was Sleeping Beauty, for God's sakes? The woman could be suffering from a concussion.

"Come on, sugar," he murmured again. Again, because he couldn't resist, he kissed her cheeks, then her lips, light, tender kisses meant to tease her back to consciousness.

Suddenly her eyelids fluttered.

"That's it," he encouraged. "Wake up."

A vague smile drifted across her face. "Thought you weren't going to do this," she said groggily.

"Do what?"

"Make love to me."

"I'm not," he said, but with far less certainty than he had only minutes before.

She sighed. "Too bad."

"Yeah," he said ruefully. "Too bad."

More confident now that she was basically okay, he lifted her into his arms and carried her back to the house. Taylor saw his father glance outside, catch sight of them, and come racing out of the house.

"What the devil's that fool woman gone and done now?"

"That horse you bought spooked," Taylor snapped back furiously. "Zelda slammed into a tree branch. I knew something like this would happen. Don't just stand there. Call the damned doctor."

Ignoring his father's stunned expression, Taylor strode inside and took Zelda straight upstairs to his old room and settled her under the covers. An instant later his mother hurried in.

"I've brought some cool water and towels. Let me just put one on her forehead. It might help with the swelling."

"I'll do it," Taylor said, brushing aside the assistance. Zelda was his responsibility. The accident could have been prevented if only he hadn't given in and taken her on that ride in the first place. Once again he'd failed to protect someone in his life.

He dipped the towel in the water, wrung it out, then pressed it gently to Zelda's forehead. "Where's the doctor?" he demanded.

His mother squeezed his shoulder reassuringly. "Sweetheart, it's only been a couple of minutes."

Minutes? It felt like an eternity. "Why isn't she awake? She was for an instant."

"Seems to me that's a good sign."

He settled on the edge of the bed next to Zelda and held tightly to her hand. Memories of those last hours in Maribeth's hospital room crowded in, filling him with panic.

"I can't lose her," he whispered, barely aware that he'd spoken aloud until he saw the look of shock, then something akin to resignation in his mother's eyes.

"You've always loved her, haven't you?" she said softly.

Taylor couldn't deal with all the ragged, raw emotions tumbling through him. Nor could he make the admission his mother was demanding. He turned back to Zelda, his hand against her cheek.

And then he prayed.

## Chapter Thirteen

Zelda felt like Sleeping Beauty, coming to in a strange place with a handsome man hovering over her. Taylor didn't look intrigued, though. He looked worried.

"What's wrong?" she whispered, wondering why her head hurt like the very devil.

"You had a run-in with a tree limb. You lost."

She touched her forehead and winced. "I lost, all right. Let me guess. A concussion."

"You seem familiar with the symptoms. Why do I suspect this isn't the first one you've had?"

"Did you forget the night we fell off Miriam Winston's roof trying to play Santa and his reindeer for her kids?"

Taylor thought back and recalled the incident all too vividly. A well-intentioned good deed gone awry. But Miriam's kids had been thrilled, she'd told them, just as the doctor came to haul them off to a hospital, where their irate parents had shouted blame back and forth.

"I remember," he told her.

"So how bad is it this time?"

"Mild, according to the doctor, but he wants you in the hospital overnight for observation."

"Where am I now?"

"In my old bedroom."

She looked around, instantly fascinated by the mementos scattered around. She managed a wobbly grin. "In your bed at last," she murmured. "Too bad I can't do anything about it."

"Yeah, too bad."

"Your parents must be thrilled. Why don't we take the doctor up on his offer and get on over to the hospital?"

"You're not budging. I told him we'd watch you all night."

"Don't you have to take Caitlin and her friends back to school?" she asked, not liking the idea of being left alone here with Beau and Geraldine Matthews, who were no doubt furious to find themselves saddled with her.

"Dad's taking the other girls back now. Caitlin refused to go. She insisted on staying right here until she sees for herself that you're okay. Threw a hellacious tantrum." He shook his head. "I can't imagine how she got to be so stubborn."

Zelda grinned. "Right."

Just then the door creaked open. Caitlin peeked around it, her face scrunched up with worry.

"Hi, sweetheart," Zelda called reassuringly. "You can come in."

Relief spread across the child's face. "You're okay?"

"My head feels as if its been used as a bowling ball, but other than that I'm just fine."

Geraldine Matthews came in on Caitlin's heels. "Sorry," she apologized. "She was determined to see for herself that you're doing better."

Zelda looked at Caitlin. "Shouldn't you have gone back to school with your friends?"

"I can go in the morning. Granddaddy said he'd take me then, unless you need me to look after you."

Taylor shook his head. "Oh, I think the rest of us can manage to look after Zelda. You don't want to miss classes, do you?"

"You have to go to work," Caitlin said stubbornly. "I could read to her. We could even play games. I know lots of good ones, like Monopoly and Scrabble and Hearts."

"Who taught you those games?" Taylor countered.

"Hey, you two," Zelda interrupted. "It won't be necessary for anyone to look after me. I'll be at work tomorrow, too."

"That's what you think," Taylor retorted.

"It really would be best to take it easy for another day," Taylor's mother said. "You're more than welcome to stay here. I'd enjoy the company."

Zelda was stunned by the unexpected sincerity of the offer. "I really don't think . . ."

"Please," she said. "It's the least we can do."

Zelda was certain there was an apology in there somewhere, but she wasn't exactly sure what it was for. The least she could do was meet the woman halfway, though how Beau Matthews would feel about all this was troublesome at best. In the end, though, it was just more rational to stay put. She had the feeling that if she budged one inch from this bed, she wasn't going to be happy with the consequences.

"If you're sure it's no bother," she said finally.

"Absolutely none," Mrs. Matthews reassured her. "Now, come along, Caitlin. Help me fix dinner. Let Zelda get some rest."

"What about Daddy?" Caitlin responded defiantly. "He's staying."

"Oh, I doubt we could get him out of there with a blast of dynamite," she retorted, to Zelda's astonishment.

When they had gone, Zelda regarded Taylor intently. "Did I miss something here?"

He shook his head, apparently equally bemused by his mother's behavior. "Maybe she's afraid of being sued," he suggested dryly. "You were on their horse when you knocked yourself out."

"She doesn't look afraid. She looks like a woman who's made up her mind about something."

"You know as much as I do," he said, staring at the now closed bedroom door with a decidedly worried expression on his face.

"Taylor?"

"Yes."

"I think I like being here in the same bed you slept in as a boy."

His lips twitched. "Do you really?"

She reached up and touched his cheek, enjoying the masculine feel of the faint stubble against her skin. "I'd like it even better if you were in here with me."

"I'm right here," he pointed out.

"That's not the same as *in* here."

He scowled at her. "You swore you were going to stop saying things like that."

"What can I tell you?" she said innocently. "That whack on the head must have addled my brain."

Suddenly his arms were under her shoulders and she found herself curled against his chest. She could feel the steady thumping of his heart. His heat seemed to envelop her and make her feel safe.

"You scared the hell out of me," he admitted eventually, his voice ragged. "You were so still out there."

"Given my reputation for nonstop energy, that would have been startling," she teased.

"It's not a joke. You could have been killed. Whatever possessed you to dig your heels into the horse's flanks?"

Zelda thought back to the precise instant when she'd acted so foolishly. "I was angry," she admitted. "I acted without thinking."

Taylor sighed. "See, that's exactly the kind of thing that terrifies me. What if you'd been killed?"

"I wasn't."

"But you might have been," he said angrily, giving her shoulders a shake. "Blast it all, aren't you ever going to learn to think first?"

She knew he was right, but she hated saying so aloud. It would only give him ammunition to use against her later, when he called things off between them one more time. "Sometimes it's as important to take risks as it is to play it safe. It's called living."

"No," he corrected softly, his expression defeated. "Sometimes it's called dying."

With that, he walked out and left her feeling miserable and more alone than ever.

Taylor wondered how many close calls one man could be expected to endure. For once, he wasn't even thinking of dangerous risks, either. He was thinking about sex. He was thinking about it too damned much, it seemed to him. One of these days, he was going to throw caution to the wind and show Zelda just how desperately he wanted her. Surely he deserved that much before he let her go again.

The trick, of course, would be letting her go once he'd known the joy of holding her in his arms, of rediscovering the satin texture of her skin, of losing himself to the scent of her, of burying himself deep inside her. He groaned.

Damn! He was aroused again. He had to stop thinking about such things. He had to concentrate on something else. Maybe a football game. All that violence and competitiveness ought to release a little pent-up sexual tension.

It didn't. Five hours later, he was bleary-eyed, exhausted, and wanted Zelda just as badly as he had before. He went upstairs and slipped into his old room. She was slung across his bed from one corner to the other, the covers kicked aside. His mother's demure little cotton nightgown might have made anyone else look almost virginal. It made Zelda look desirable.

In his current state of perpetual lust, sackcloth would have made Zelda look desirable.

A pale shaft of moonlight streamed in the window and made her skin shimmer like candlelight on silk. He closed his eyes as if that could stop the wave of pure longing that swept through him.

He'd be okay, he told himself firmly. He'd escape before he did anything foolish, if only she didn't stir sensuously, if only she didn't awaken.

She did both. She came awake slowly, sensuously, her gaze instantly locking with his in a way that made his pulse hammer. She stretched, pulling the fabric of that innocent gown taut across her breasts, hiking it above her knees and drawing his attention from the relative safety of bare calves to the pure temptation of that shadowy mound between her thighs. A faint, satisfied smile curved her lips and still he thought he might escape.

Then she lifted her arms, deliberately inviting him, tempting him.

One mortal man could withstand only so much, he thought with a groan as he walked slowly to the door and locked it. His return was even slower, drawing out the anticipation, trying not to acknowledge how one lone woman could scramble his wits.

"This is a bad idea," he murmured, even as he lowered himself onto the bed.

"No," she said, boldly lifting the gown over her head. "This is right. It's always been right."

She was beautiful. That was his one last completely rational thought. Then all that mattered was the way she felt beneath his caress, the way she responded when his lips closed over a nipple and drew it into his mouth, the way her hips seemed to seek his. She was all fire and passion in bed as she was in life, taunting him, inflaming him, luring him.

"Sweet," he murmured as he tasted her skin.

"Taylor, I need you now," she insisted. "Now."

"Not yet," he taunted her. "You don't get your way in everything. We're going to take this at a nice, slow, leisurely pace. It's taken us ten years to get here. I'm not about to rush it."

She bucked beneath him, her skin already damp with perspiration. "Couldn't we try for slow and leisurely next time?" she whispered, lifting his shirt and raking her fingers along his belly. His belt buckle provided only a temporary slowdown in her determined assault. When it was undone, she moved on to the zipper of his jeans. The slow rasp as she pulled it down was pure torment.

"If you keep that up, we'll have to," he said, his whole body aching with the effort of maintaining control.

"You have on too many clothes."

"Self-defense."

She slid down, latched onto the cuffs of his jeans and tugged. Taylor was impressed by her determination. He allowed her to shuck them off, then moaned as she scattered little kisses all the way back up his legs. His breath snagged in his throat as her mouth skimmed over him, her pace fast, her intent clear.

When she reached his mouth, he ended the game, claiming her with a kiss that started out hard and punishing and gentled into something sweet and tender and heart-stoppingly familiar. He recognized then that this moment had been inevitable, that no matter what came after, they had been destined to be in each other's arms again.

And he wanted to savor it, to do all the sensual, exciting things he'd been imagining—remembering—for months, maybe even years. But that wouldn't happen, if they didn't slow down. This fire inside him would blaze out of control. She deserved better than that.

He tempered the kiss, then rolled onto his back. Unfortunately, she came with him. In less than a heartbeat, she was astride him, her face radiant with satisfaction, her red hair cascading to her shoulders in a tangle of curls.

"I see patience is not one of your virtues," he said, his voice coming in a ragged gasp as she settled over him. His arousal strained against his cotton briefs, which were scanty protection against her tempting heat. His whole body throbbed with need. Her gaze locked with his, she wriggled against him in a slow, provocative rhythm, and Taylor was lost.

He somehow managed to scramble out of his briefs with her willing assistance and then she was poised above him again. With careful deliberation, she settled herself over him, taking him deep inside until he was surrounded by that tight, moist, velvet heat. Tears shimmered on her lashes.

"Zelda? Is something wrong?"

"I'm sorry, but I couldn't . . . I couldn't let you change your mind again," she told him.

"I wouldn't have, not this time. It's too late for that. I think maybe it was too late the first time I ever saw you."

She rode him then, as she had ridden that horse—with wild abandon, unaware of the dangers, lost to everything except pure sensation. As time disappeared and need consumed him, Taylor thought for one fleeting instant that he had discovered something new and magical. Then he realized it was as old as time. It was the freedom to enjoy all that life had to offer, to love with everything in him.

He also knew, as their bodies stilled and passion ebbed, that it couldn't last. It never did.

Floating on a cloud of pure sensation, Zelda thought that nothing could ever be this perfect again. She had known the precise instant when Taylor had given himself up to the emotions, had seen the exultant expression on his face and gloried in it.

But just as she felt the sweetness of triumph, she realized he was slipping away from her and he was doing it intentionally. Though Taylor's arms remained tight around her, she sensed that something indefinable had shifted.

"What is it?" she asked, smoothing that untamable lock of hair from his forehead.

"Nothing."

"Don't tell me nothing. I know you, Taylor Matthews." She recalled what Sarah Lynn had told her. "According to some, I even know you better than you know yourself."

"Meaning?"

"Meaning that you love me, always have, always will." She said it with utter confidence, hiding the doubts that his stiff, unyielding demeanor stirred in her.

To his credit, he didn't deny it. That made it that much worse when he said, "It doesn't matter."

Zelda slowly extricated herself from his embrace, exchanging heated comfort for cold loneliness. "What do you mean, it doesn't matter? It's the only thing that matters."

"You asked me about my marriage."

"That was weeks ago. I've figured out most of it by now."

"I don't want you relying on conjecture. I want you to hear all of it, from me."

Bringing Maribeth into this bed was the last thing Zelda wanted, but she could hardly stop him from answering questions she herself had plagued him with.

"After you were gone, after I'd driven you off, I was in a lousy mood for months," he began. "I didn't want to hear from my parents that I'd made the right decision. I missed you so badly, I think I went a little crazy. When Maribeth was paraded before me as the perfect candidate for the wife of a man destined for politics, I didn't much care. She was sweet and lovely and more than willing, though why she'd take on a man who was still hung up on another woman is beyond me."

"She knew about me?"

"I told her every chance I got. Maybe I was just trying to scare her off. Anyway, after the wedding, I tried my damnedest to make it work, but you were there between us, and she knew it. She began to drink. And when she drank she did things, totally reckless, out-of-character things."

"Why?"

"I wondered that, but because I was so damned afraid that I already knew the answer, I didn't ask the question, not until it was too late, anyway." He regarded Zelda bleakly. "Do you want to hear what she admitted eventually? She told me that she knew she was a disappointment to me. She said she wanted to be more like you so that I would love her as much as I loved you."

"Oh, dear Lord," Zelda whispered, trying to imagine the kind of desperation and pain behind such an admission. "Oh, Taylor, how terrible for her. And for you."

"Me? Don't pity me. I got exactly what I deserved, enough guilt to last a lifetime and then some. I've seen firsthand what recklessness and love can lead a person to do. So if you want to stick around for more sex, if you want to stay on at the office, I'm not strong enough to deny myself the pleasure of that, but as for love, as for commitment, I can't do it."

He looked her straight in the eye, and Zelda felt all the hope drain right out of her.

"I won't do it," he emphasized, just in case she hadn't gotten the message. "I won't get tangled up with all that recklessness again. I know how it ends up."

Foolishly Zelda had thought of tonight as a turning point, linking passion and respect in a way that could endure for a lifetime. She still believed with all her heart that it could, but not if Taylor kept clinging to the past and refused to see the possibilities.

That meant she was going to have to fight with everything left in her. At least now she had some idea what she was up against.

## Chapter Fourteen

"Would you say that one more time?" Zelda said very slowly.

Taylor hardened himself against the hurt in her eyes. He couldn't allow himself to forget for one single instant that appearances could be deceiving. He'd learned that from Maribeth, too late to save their marriage, too late to save her life.

It was true that for weeks now Zelda had been acting more responsibly than he'd remembered. He'd never had a better assistant, in fact. She was organized and efficient, intelligent and clever when it came to helping him with cases. But then, just yesterday on that damned horse she'd lost her temper and done something exceptionally foolish. He couldn't trust her not to do that kind of thing again. And again.

Worse, he seemed to be the one who brought out her impetuous nature. He always had. Hell, at one time he'd been even more of a danger junkie than she was, but he'd learned. Now no one could accuse him of being anything but steady and dependable. He shook off the word *boring* when it popped into his head. *Responsible.*

"I was just trying to explain why it will never work between us," he said carefully. "I know what you're like, Zelda. There's a reckless streak inside you that nothing will ever tame."

"A reckless streak," she repeated as if she'd never heard the phrase before. Fire sparked in her eyes. "Maybe I just call it living, Taylor. Maybe I see it as grabbing life and hanging on for all it's worth. Maybe I don't want to cruise through my years on this earth in neutral, letting things pass me by."

She glared at him. "And that includes love."

*Love.* The word resounded in his head, promising so much. He knew all too well, though, what sins could be committed in the name of love, what tragedies could occur.

"This isn't about love," he said quietly, hoping the denial would silence his own doubts, maybe make him feel more at peace with the choice he was making. He knew in his gut, though, that it was a lousy choice, no better this time than it had been before. He clung to it stubbornly just the same.

"Yes, it is about love. And if you tell me to go this time, it will be for good," she threatened in a low tone that revealed more fury with each word. "I won't waste one single minute mourning you again. I won't waste one single ounce of energy thinking about what we could have had together. You will no longer exist for me. Have you got that, Taylor Matthews?"

A great empty space opened up inside him. He could already feel the void her going would create in his life and he wondered if anything ever again would hurt so much. He fought the urge to drag her back into his arms. With every last ounce of sanity he had left, he made himself regard her calmly, emotionlessly.

"I've got it," he said softly. "It doesn't change anything."

He watched as the passionate spirit seemed to drain right out of her, and he hated himself for causing it. Still, that defiant chin of hers lifted a notch. A brief flash of anger darkened her eyes to the shade of a turbulent sea. Zelda would be okay. She had a survivalist's instincts. He wondered if he would do nearly as well.

Something cold and lonely settled over him as he watched her slide from his bed, her shoulders stiff with pride. She dragged a sheet with her and wrapped it around herself like a protective cloak.

Without glancing in his direction, she said, "I'll be out of your way in a minute."

"Zelda..." His voice trailed off as uncertainty swept through him.

She paused, but didn't turn around. As he watched her waiting for him to say whatever it was he'd begun, he thought he knew what it must be like in hell. He owed her better than this, but too many things had happened. He didn't have anything better left in him, just regrets.

"Nothing," he said finally. "I was just going to say there's no need to rush. My parents expect you to be here in the morning."

She trembled then as if a draft had chilled her, but he knew better. Her spine went ramrod straight as she walked into the bathroom and quietly closed the door.

Feeling more bereft than he ever had in his life, Taylor cursed softly and climbed from the bed where only hours ago he'd rediscovered magic, the same bed where he'd spent his entire adolescence dreaming of what it would be like to possess Zelda the way he had tonight. As he pulled on a pair of jeans and an old sweatshirt, he tried to reassure himself that he'd had no choice, but the words seemed hollow.

In the kitchen he made a pot of coffee and waited. The slow, methodical click of the clock over the sink marked the agony of waiting. He heard the shower stop, then, after a while, the opening of the bathroom door. All the while his imagination taunted him with images of Zelda's skin, soft and flushed from the steam, smelling of something sweetly exotic.

When she finally came into the room, his heart wrenched at the bleak expression on her face. She'd tugged her hair back into a ponytail and pulled his baseball cap on again. She looked about seventeen, until he sought her gaze and saw the weariness and pain of someone much older.

"I'm going to stop by the office when I leave here, to pick up my things," she said.

"Just like that?" he said without thinking. "Sorry. Of course."

"Will you be coming in tomorrow?"

He shook his head. "I have a meeting in Charleston. I won't be back until late tomorrow."

"Then I'll see if Darlene can work."

A thoughtful gesture under the circumstances, he admitted. *Responsible.* There was that word again. "Thank you."

He sat there, just staring at her, as if he had to absorb everything about her in the next few seconds, enough to last a lifetime. She looked unhappy and uneasy.

"I need to borrow your car to get home," she said finally.

He shook his head. "You're in no condition to drive. I'll get my keys and take you home."

"I'd rather you wouldn't. Just lend me the car. I can drive myself."

Irrationally annoyed by her desire to leave alone, he snapped, "I said I'd drive you. I'll be out in a minute."

He went upstairs and snatched his keys off the dresser, then paused long enough to write a note to his parents explaining that Zelda had felt she'd be more comfortable in her own home.

Outside, he found her already sitting in the car, scrunched against the passenger door as if she couldn't quite bear to be so much as a single inch closer. He opened his mouth to say something, anything, to end the silence, but words wouldn't come.

In front of her house, she stilled his move to get out with a single gesture. "I'll be fine."

He bit back an argument. "Call me if you need anything."

"I won't." She regarded him coolly. "Well, then, I guess this is goodbye."

"Zelda, I'm sorry it didn't work out." He struggled with the apology, knowing it wasn't enough, angry with himself for putting them both through this anguish for a second time.

A rueful smile tugged at her lips. "I'm sorry you didn't even give it a chance."

And then, before he could think of a single thing to say to that, she was out of the car, down the walk and inside with the door firmly closed behind her. Only then did Taylor know with absolute certainty that she had taken his heart with her.

"The man is an idiot," Zelda declared emphatically as she threw her personal belongings into a box that had once held computer paper. It was amazing how much a person could accumulate in a few short weeks. Makeup, hair brushes, a toothbrush, a letter opener that could serve as a dandy murder weapon, she noted as she tossed it into the box. Then, of course, there was her broken heart. Not many people got to walk away from a job with one of those.

"Damn him!"

She tried to tell herself that she'd given it her best shot this time. It sure as hell wasn't her fault that things had fallen apart. It was Taylor and his stubborn decision to bury himself right along with that miserable wife of his. That's what he was doing, of course, paying penance for who-knew-what crimes he thought he'd committed. His declaration earlier had absolutely nothing to do with her and everything to do with the bushel of guilt he was hauling around.

All of which might be true, Zelda conceded, but where did that get her? On a fast jet back to L.A., that's where. Will or no will, she was going. First thing in the morning, if at all possible. She'd been wasting time with this futile attempt to recapture the past.

She was already reaching for the phone to make a reservation, when it rang. She hesitated. Who would be calling Taylor at the office at this ungodly hour? She'd waited until the end of the day, when Darlene would be gone, before stopping by to pick up her things. She'd made sure that Taylor's car was nowhere around before using her key to let herself in.

It was nearly seven o'clock now, too late for the usual business calls. Obviously this was someone who knew Taylor's workaholic habits, she decided.

Constitutionally unable to ignore a ringing phone, especially one as persistent as this, Zelda finally picked it up.

"Taylor Matthews's office."

"This is Ms. Patterson at Graystone School," the cultured voice that Zelda readily recognized said. "Is Mr. Matthews there by any chance? I've already tried him at home."

Zelda's pulse kicked into overdrive. "No, he's gone to Charleston. Is Caitlin okay? Is there anything I can do?"

"She's not feeling well. Her grandfather just brought her back this morning and she became ill around lunchtime. It's nothing to be alarmed about, I'm sure, but she is running a high fever. Our doctor here has taken a look at her and thinks it's just a touch of the flu. We could keep her in the infirmary, of course, but I thought she might be more comfortable at home."

"I'll be there in an hour," Zelda said without hesitation. She had no idea how Taylor would feel about her going after Caitlin under the circumstances, but right this instant she didn't give a damn.

"Actually, Mr. Matthews really should be the one to come."

"He's not available."

"Caitlin's grandparents, then."

"Really, there's no need to bother them. I'll leave a message for Mr. Matthews with his service, but you and I both know he would want his daughter back here as quickly as possible. I can come right away. That way she'll be home when he gets back."

Ms. Patterson continued to hesitate. If they weren't wasting precious time, Zelda might have admired her for the caution.

"Well, he did give permission for you to pick her up once before," she said finally. "I suppose it would be all right."

"I will take full responsibility for the decision," Zelda reassured her.

She drove with the accelerator pressed all the way to the floor and made it to Graystone in less than an hour. Ms. Patterson was waiting for her in the foyer. "Come with me. Caitlin's in the infirmary. I've told her you were on the way."

At the doorway to the large, sterile room with its gleaming medical equipment and row of beds, Zelda paused and drew in a deep breath. Caitlin was the only child in the room and she was huddled under the covers, her complexion almost as white as the sheets except for the feverish, too bright splashes of color on her cheeks. A momentary panic raced through Zelda. What if she botched this? She'd never nursed a sick child before.

Caitlin's whispery voice cut through her chaotic thoughts.

"Zelda, I hurt," she cried miserably. "I want to go home."

Zelda reached her side in an instant and brushed a lock of hair from her forehead. Her skin was burning up, she realized with alarm. Still, she somehow managed to keep her voice even and reassuring. "I know you do, sweetheart. Let's bundle you up and take you home to your own bed. I'll bet you'll feel lots better as soon as you're there."

"I've packed her bag for her," Ms. Patterson said. "It's in the foyer. Just give her lots of fluids, and I'm sure she'll be just fine. If her temperature goes up any more, give the doctor a call. I've put his number in her suitcase."

Zelda nodded. "Then I guess we're all set," she said cheerfully. She scooped Caitlin up into her arms, prepared to struggle with the unaccustomed weight. Instead, she was startled by how light and fragile she felt.

Once she had Caitlin settled on the back seat of the car with a blanket wrapped securely around her, Zelda slid behind the wheel. "You okay back there?"

"I'm hot," Caitlin said, squirming restlessly.

"Don't toss the blanket off, sweetheart. You'll get chilled and then you'll only feel worse."

Aware of the precious cargo she was carrying, Zelda drove far more cautiously on the way home. It seemed to take forever. By the time she pulled into Taylor's driveway, her shoulders were stiff with tension. The thought of going back into that house, of seeing Taylor again after what had happened only hours before made her almost physically ill, but she managed to steel herself against the memory. Right now, Caitlin was the only thing that mattered.

She carried the listless child to her room and tucked her beneath the covers. Downstairs she found a pitcher of fresh orange juice. She filled another with cool water and took both containers upstairs. She grabbed a washcloth from the bathroom.

"Here you go, sweetheart," she said. "I've brought you some juice."

Caitlin shook her head. "I don't want any."

"How about some water, then? You need to drink something."

"No. Where's Daddy?"

"He'll be home in a little while. He had to go to Charleston earlier. He'll be back as soon as he gets the message that you're here. Why don't we take your temperature and see if that fever's down at all?"

It was a hundred and three. Zelda nearly panicked. What was normal? Ninety-eight point six? Wasn't anything over a hundred dangerous? Why the hell couldn't she remember? Forcing herself to remain calm, she went into the hallway and used the portable phone to call the doctor.

"No need for alarm," he reassured her in a voice that had clearly soothed hundreds of overwrought mothers. "Children tend to get very high temperatures, much higher than adults. Still, I wouldn't want to see this climbing any more. Keep her on fluids. Sponge her off with cool water. Give me the number there, and I'll check back with you in a couple of hours. If anything changes significantly before that, don't hesitate to call me. I'll drive on over, if need be.''

Zelda tried to imagine a doctor in Los Angeles being quite so responsive and couldn't. In her experience most of them were overworked, impatient and in serious need of training in bedside manners.

''Thank you,'' she said. ''This is all a little new to me. I'm just filling in until her father gets back.''

''And you're terrified something will go wrong on your watch,'' he said. ''Well, we'll just have to see that doesn't happen. Now, you go on back to your patient. I'm here if you need me.''

Eventually, to Zelda's relief, Caitlin's temperature seemed to stabilize, no better, but no worse, either. She'd fallen asleep and had managed to kick off all the covers. Zelda replaced them, then sank down in a chair beside the bed and watched her sleep, alert to every hitch in her breathing, every soft sigh, every restless shifting of her body.

Where the devil was Taylor? she wondered again and again as the hours dragged on. Caitlin kept rousing, asking for her daddy, then drifting back into a restless sleep. Zelda talked to the doctor twice more, reassured by his calm demeanor and Caitlin's unchanged condition.

"Oh, baby," she murmured as her cool fingers caressed a burning cheek. She picked up the damp washcloth and sponged Caitlin's forehead. She opened her eyes slowly as if even that much movement hurt.

"How're you feeling?" Zelda asked.

"I'm hot."

"I know, sweetheart. The cool water should bring your fever down soon."

"Can I sit in your lap in the rocker?"

"Absolutely," she said, gathering her up and settling into the rocking chair. Caitlin snuggled closer. "Better?"

"Uh-huh."

"Good." She rocked slowly, holding this child of the man she loved more than life itself. Longing spread through her, followed by the sharp anguish of knowing that she would never share Caitlin or other children with Taylor. These moments, however fleeting, would be all she'd have.

Taylor had never in his entire life had more of a desire to get rip-roaring drunk. Naturally, he didn't. He'd ordered a double bourbon straight up and swirled it around in the glass for the past hour. The bartender had probably never seen anyone nurse a drink the way Taylor was.

"Something wrong with the drink?" he asked finally.

"No."

Worry etched a frown on the man's expressive face. "You trying to kick a habit?"

Taylor's laughter was mirthless. "Something like that, but not what you think."

"Ah, woman trouble," the bartender guessed. He took Taylor's untouched drink and replaced it with a cup of coffee. "Want to talk about it?"

"There's nothing to talk about," Taylor said. "She's gone. I sent her away. That's that."

"Having a change of heart?"

"No. Absolutely not," Taylor said adamantly.

A disbelieving grin spread across the bartender's face. "Hey, I was just asking."

"Sorry."

"Maybe you ought to think about changing your mind, though. In my experience, when a woman has a man all tied up in knots, the only way to get her out of his system is to play it through to the end."

"Didn't work."

"Then you didn't get to the end, did you?"

Taylor appreciated the amateur analysis, but in his opinion the guy couldn't have been further off the mark. His relationship with Zelda was definitely at the end of the road. He drained the last of the coffee and tossed a couple of bills onto the bar. The bartender shoved them back.

"The coffee and the pep talk are on me this time."

"I can't let you do that."

"Sure you can. Just come in sometime and let me know how it turns out."

"Yeah, right. I'll invite you to the wedding," he said dryly.

He drove to an inn in the heart of old Charleston and checked in. He couldn't see one single reason to go back to Port William tonight. With any luck Zelda would be gone by morning and temptation would be out of his life once and for all. The prospect didn't bring him much satisfaction.

He flipped on the TV, took a shower and settled down to read the depositions he'd picked up earlier in the day. The words blurred on the page, and his concentration was shot. The background noise from the television irritated him. He finally switched it off.

Wide awake and determined not to think about Zelda and that soft, vulnerable look in her eyes, he decided he'd call his service one last time.

"Mr. Matthews, thank goodness," Wilma said. "You need to get yourself one of them beepers."

"Why, when I have you?"

"It's your girl, sir."

His heartbeat seemed to skid to a stop. "Caitlin?"

"Yes, sir. Your secretary..."

Secretary? He didn't have one anymore. "Darlene?"

"No, the new one. Miss Zelda. She called earlier this evening and said Caitlin was taken sick at school."

A sense of unreality spread through him. Dread had his pulse hammering. "I'll leave right away.

Could you call over there and tell them I'm leaving Charleston now?''

"She's not at the school. Miss Zelda went and picked her up. She's at home. Checked on her myself not more than an hour ago. Her fever hasn't broken yet, but the doctor told Miss Zelda not to worry. Kids spike these fevers all the time. I have four young ones of my own. Every one of them scared the bejesus out of me a time or two. Don't you go driving too fast to get home, you hear?''

"Thanks, Wilma.''

It took Taylor less than ten minutes to dress, pack up his briefcase and get on the road. For the first time in his life, he wished he had a car phone so he could call and see for himself that Caitlin was not seriously ill. He hadn't wanted to waste a single second making that call before leaving the hotel.

She's with Zelda, he reminded himself. Whatever his doubts about Zelda and about their own future, he knew she would die herself before she allowed anything to happen to his daughter. Given everything else he knew about her, he wasn't sure why he felt so strongly about this, but he believed it with all his heart.

## Chapter Fifteen

It was after midnight when Taylor finally pulled into the driveway at home. Every light in the house seemed to be burning. Why? What had gone wrong? He took off for the front door at a dead run, not certain what he expected to find inside. Doctors? Paramedics? His parents? All foolish thoughts given the lack of a single vehicle in front of the house other than his own and Zelda's bright red convertible.

He opened the door quietly, then listened. There wasn't so much as a faint sound of stirring anywhere. Encouraged by that, he took a quick survey of the downstairs rooms, his mouth dropping open at the mess in the kitchen. Apparently Zelda had tried to fix something to tempt Caitlin's appetite.

Judging from the chaos, it had taken several attempts.

Frozen juice cans littered the sink. Eggshells, a tin of cinnamon and an empty milk carton hinted at an attempt to make custard, which he could have told her was a waste of time. Two pieces of burned toast remained in the toaster as if she'd just taken one look at them and given up that idea. A smile tugged at his mouth. He had to give her high marks for determination, anyway.

He flipped off the kitchen light, dismissing the mess until morning, then climbed the stairs. Up here, the bathroom and hall lights were on, though only a faint glow showed from Caitlin's room. Her nightlight. She wouldn't sleep without it. Had she told Zelda or had Zelda guessed?

He walked quietly down the hall and stepped into the dimly lit room, his glance going straight to the bed. It was empty.

Then he looked at the rocking chair, one Maribeth had bought when Caitlin was a baby and which Caitlin had climbed in herself from the first day she could reach it, content to rock for hours. What he saw now brought a lump to his throat. Emotions he hadn't wanted to feel, had thought he could dismiss, crowded in as he studied the two people who were most precious to him in all the world. One of them, his daughter, he had a right to love, a duty to protect. The other was a woman he had to force himself to sacrifice, for all their sakes.

Zelda was sound asleep. Exhaustion had left faint shadows under her eyes. The bump on her forehead had turned an interesting combination of purple and yellow. Though Zelda had to have been in pain herself, Caitlin was cradled protectively in her arms, wrapped in a blanket, the thumb she hadn't sucked in years tucked in her mouth.

He crept into the room and knelt beside them. He brushed his fingertips across Caitlin's brow and discovered it was cool to the touch. A profound relief spread through him. She was okay. Zelda had seen to it. Even as angry as she must be with him, she had cared for Caitlin. He would be forever in her debt for that.

His daughter stirred. Blue eyes sleepily sought his. "Hi, Daddy. I've been sick."

"So I heard," he whispered, indicating Zelda's sleeping form. "How're you feeling now?"

"I'm all better. Zelda made me custard."

He grinned. "I thought you hated custard."

"That was your custard," she said imperiously. "Zelda's was good."

"I see." He reached out to pick her up. "Let's get you into bed. It's late."

"But I've been sleeping and sleeping."

"It's one in the morning. A little more sleep will do you good."

"What about Zelda?"

Just then Zelda's eyes blinked open. Her gaze met Taylor's then skittered away. Instantly she touched her hand to Caitlin's forehead. The worried expression on her face disappeared.

"The fever's gone," she pronounced with evident relief. "How do you feel, pumpkin?"

Caitlin rolled her eyes at the nickname she barely tolerated from Taylor or his parents. "Better. I told Daddy you make the best custard of anybody. Is there any left?"

"I made enough for an army," Zelda admitted. "The refrigerator is filled with it."

"Can I have more?"

"Now?" Zelda asked incredulously. "It's the middle of the night."

"But I'm hungry. I'll bet Daddy is, too."

"I did miss dinner," Taylor confessed. "How about you?"

"I wasn't especially hungry," Zelda admitted.

"Then that does it. Custard all around," he said, then scowled at his daughter. "Then you, my little one, are going back to sleep."

"Can we eat downstairs?" Caitlin asked, already scrambling out of Zelda's embrace and darting for the door. Her flu or whatever it had been evidently forgotten.

Taylor didn't miss the expression of sadness that suddenly stole over Zelda's face. He knew how it felt to be suddenly bereft. He waited for her at the top of the stairs, then touched her hand. "Thank you. I'll never forget what you did."

"I did it for Caitlin," she said stiffly, still refusing to look directly at him.

He touched her chin, forcing her to meet his gaze. "I know that," he said softly. "I'm grateful just the same. Maybe more than you can possibly imagine."

Seeing the gratitude in Taylor's eyes, the sudden warmth, Zelda felt her spirits slowly begin to lift. It was going to be okay, after all. She was almost sure of it.

Almost.

It was that one tiny shred of uncertainty that made her cautious. Convictions held for as long as Taylor had clung to his about her didn't turn around overnight. She'd learned that lesson just a day or two ago to her bitter dismay. But surely after these tense hours when Caitlin had been left in her care he had seen indisputable evidence of the woman she'd become, not the reckless girl he remembered. Surely that would count for something, she thought, then hated herself for placing her emotions at his mercy.

"Will you read me another story?" Caitlin pleaded just then, interrupting Zelda's thoughts.

Zelda smiled at her. She had agreed to stay on for another day or two until the doctor gave Caitlin permission to return to school.

"Which one do you want?" she asked. She'd been reading *Little House on the Prairie* for hours already. She'd re-read all of *Angelina Ballerina* at least a dozen times, as well.

"The ballerina one," Caitlin said this time. "I asked Daddy if I could have ballet lessons."

"And what did he say?"

"He said when I get well we'd talk about it. Do you think he'll let me? It would mean moving back home."

Zelda was surprised that Taylor hadn't dismissed the idea out of hand. He'd never been willing to bring Caitlin home before. "If your father said he'd consider it, then I'm sure he will."

Caitlin regarded her intently. "He'd need someone to help him, if I came home," she said slyly.

Zelda glanced into guileless blue eyes. "Oh?"

"You could do it. He already likes you. You don't have a little girl of your own at home, so I could be your little girl and then I'd have a mommy and a daddy."

Zelda wiped at the tear that tumbled down her cheek at the ingenuous suggestion. She couldn't even bring herself to look at Caitlin. Suddenly she felt two little arms go around her neck. She heard a faint sniff.

"I'm sorry," Caitlin whispered. "I didn't mean to make you sad."

Zelda hugged her. "Oh, baby, knowing that you'd like me to be your mommy doesn't make me sad. It's the nicest thing anybody's ever said to me."

"Then why are you crying?"

"Oh, just grown-up foolishness."

"Does that mean I can tell Daddy you'll do it?"

Zelda chuckled at Caitlin's persistence. "No, you may not. I think this is one situation you'll have to leave entirely up to your father to handle," she said, regretting more than she could say that she couldn't encourage Caitlin to give the bullheaded man a gentle shove.

To Zelda's astonishment, Taylor did agree to let Caitlin stay at home until after the holidays. Maybe her bout with the flu, as mild as it had been, had awakened him to the fact that she ought to be home where he could look after her. He promised the school he would hire a tutor to see that she kept up with her lessons. Just as he hung up the phone after working out the details with Ms. Patterson, Zelda heard herself volunteering to do it. It was amazing how little relationship there was between her brain and her tongue.

Taylor's startled gaze clashed with hers. "I thought you were leaving."

She shrugged. "I'm in no rush. Christmas is less than a month away. I can always go back to Los Angeles after New Year's."

"If you're going to stick around, you could keep your job with me," he suggested, his gaze fixed on her as if he were trying to gauge her reaction. "That would make more sense."

"I don't think so."

"Afraid to be in the same room with me?" he taunted.

"You're the one who ought to panic at the thought," she said dryly. "You know what everyone says about my temper."

"You're a pushover," he contradicted. "Anyone who can read the same book over and over and over without screaming is an old softie."

"Then let me keep on doing that," she said. "There's no point in hiring a stranger for just a few weeks."

Still, Taylor hesitated. It finally dawned on Zelda why.

"You don't trust me with her, do you?" she said, swallowing hard against the hurt that seemed lodged in her throat.

"Of course I do," he said too quickly.

Zelda regarded him belligerently. "Then prove it."

"This isn't some game of I-dare-you," he chided.

"No," she agreed softly. "It's far more important than any game we've ever played. It's a matter of trust and respect."

"It's a matter of my child's well-being."

"Damn it, Taylor, don't you realize that I would protect your daughter with my life? You know what happened just days ago. It might have turned into something more serious, but it didn't. I watched over her every second. I stayed in constant touch with the doctor."

A sigh shuddered through him. "I know that. Deep in my gut I don't question that at all, but up here..." He tapped his head. "Up here, I keep seeing her mother's car at the bottom of that ravine. But for the grace of God, Caitlin could have been in it with her. And no one loved our daughter more than Maribeth did."

*"I am not Maribeth!"* Zelda snapped, then threw up her hands in a gesture of surrender. "Why am I doing this? How many times will I allow you to humiliate me with your unreasonable doubts? I can't prove something to a man who won't even see what's right in front of him." She grabbed her coat. "I'm out of here. Kiss Caitlin for me and tell her I love her and that I'll miss her."

Shaking with anger, she was all the way through the front door and on the porch before she felt Taylor's fingers lock around her wrist. Though his expression was still filled with doubts, he said quietly, "Go upstairs and tell her you'll be helping with her tutoring for a while."

"Go to hell," she retorted, wrenching free.

"Don't punish Caitlin for my stupidity."

The plea reached her as nothing else might have. Caitlin wanted so badly to be back at home again. Could she deny her this chance to live at home like a normal little girl again? Perhaps by the end of the holidays, Taylor would see that Caitlin was where she belonged, at home with him. It could be her gift to the little girl she'd come to love.

"I'll be here first thing in the morning," she agreed finally. "After you've left for work."

Taylor's expression hardened, but he nodded. "Fine."

"I'll stay until you get home in the evenings, but not one second longer. Understood?"

He sighed. "Yes, Zelda. The ground rules are perfectly clear."

She looked into his eyes, hoping to see something that would make this easier, but all she saw was a man who had to struggle to trust her. She hated him for that. More, she hated herself for sticking around for this one pitiful crumb he'd deigned to toss her. Only Caitlin's welfare allowed her to live with the decision.

It might not have been so awful spending her days with Caitlin and avoiding Taylor, if it hadn't been Christmastime. It was a season for joy, a season for families and forgiveness, her very favorite time of year.

It was also a season for the worst loneliness of Zelda's life. She felt cut off from everyone she loved, especially Taylor, and he was close by.

She bought presents for Kate and her other friends in Los Angeles and mailed them off. Suddenly she longed to be back there, to be back in a job where she was respected and trusted, back in a place where she felt a part of things, rather than an outsider, always wanting what she couldn't have. In L.A. anything was possible. She resolved to go back immediately after the first of the year. She would talk to Kate soon and set the wheels in motion for her return.

In the meantime, Caitlin wanted to go Christmas shopping for her father, and Zelda had promised to take her.

"What are you going to get Daddy?" Caitlin asked as they strolled through the mall looking in every decorated window. Carols blared over the loudspeaker system. Santa Claus sat in a winter wonderland display, listening patiently to children's wish lists. Despite their mission, she was having the time of her life. Her depression began to lift.

"I hadn't really thought about it," Zelda said. "We probably won't exchange gifts."

"He's already bought yours," Caitlin confided.

Zelda was startled by the revelation. "Oh?"

"I'm not supposed to tell what it is."

"Then I guess you'd better keep it a secret."

Caitlin looked disappointed by Zelda's refusal to plague her with questions. The truth was, Zelda didn't want to know what impersonal little trinket Taylor might have bought for her. A scarf, probably. Something he'd had Darlene pick out, now that she was working in the office for him again until he could locate another replacement.

"Now, then," Zelda said briskly. "Have you decided what you want to get him?"

"He said he needs a new shirt. A white dress shirt," Caitlin said. She glanced up at Zelda. "I think that sounds awfully dull."

"I agree," Zelda said, suddenly grinning. "Let's choose a shirt with a little pizzazz for him."

Caitlin regarded her uncertainly. "What's *pizzazz*?"

"Trust me."

"He said white."

"What does he know? He's a man." She led Caitlin to the men's department and zeroed in on a table filled with shirts with stripes, colored shirts with white collars and French cuffs. There wasn't a plain white shirt in the lot.

Caitlin immediately reached for one with gray stripes. Zelda would have picked something besides gray, but it definitely had more pizzazz than Taylor's usual selections. She picked one in mauve and gray. Despite her reservations, Caitlin's eyes lit up.

"These are definitely better than white, but I can't afford two."

"You get the gray stripes. I'll get the mauve. Now let's look at ties." She found a couple that were classic in design, but done with more fashionable colors. She draped two choices over the shirts. "What do you think?"

"Beautiful," Caitlin said. "Do you really think Daddy will like them, though?"

"I think he'll hate them...at first. You'll just have to keep telling him how handsome he looks," she said, thinking it was too bad she wouldn't be there on Christmas morning to tell him herself.

Maybe she would even go back to Los Angeles before Christmas, she thought, unable to stop the tiny sigh of regret that eased through her. It might be a miserable, lonely holiday there, but in Port William it was guaranteed to be hell.

## Chapter Sixteen

"Kate, I'm coming back," Zelda announced when she reached her boss in Los Angeles early on Christmas Eve morning. "Do I still have a job?"

There was a slight hesitation. "Of course, you have a job," Kate said finally. "But, Zelda, what about the will? What about this man you mentioned, the one you've always loved?"

"None of that matters," she lied. "I'll relinquish everything in my mother's estate. As for any man in my life, I think you'd better call up Brandon Halloran and tell him he can meddle in my love life as much as he pleases."

Kate chuckled. "He'll be delighted to hear that. I think he's been bored since he got me married off.

He's been making noises about trying to find someone for Sammy, his granddaughter-in-law's brother. The poor kid is terrified. He's barely twenty. Jason and Dana say that Sammy's threatening to disown them all if Brandon so much as invites one eligible girl to dinner. He'd be forever indebted to you for providing a distraction.''

She paused, then asked, ''Zelda, do you want to tell me what's really going on back there?''

Zelda sighed at the evident concern. ''Nothing that won't be forgotten as soon as I get back to Los Angeles.''

''Okay, if you say so, but remember that I'm a good listener.''

''I know that. I'll call you when I have my travel details worked out.''

''Will you stay there through the holidays at least?''

''No. I'm going to try to get out of here tonight or tomorrow.''

''On Christmas day?'' Kate said, sounding horrified. She drew in a breath. ''Never mind. If you get back tonight or tomorrow, you'll have Christmas dinner with us. No need to even call first. Just show up about four-thirty. Promise me now.''

''I promise,'' Zelda said, already feeling as if her life was getting back on track. It would be fun to share Christmas dinner with a family, even if it was the wrong family.

When she'd hung up, Zelda walked slowly through the house in which she'd grown up. She wouldn't miss it, wouldn't miss anything about Port William, in fact. She was grateful her mother had forced her to come back. She'd definitely put a few ghosts to rest, not the least of them her love for Taylor. She could finally stop clinging to that as an excuse for avoiding new relationships. Nope, there was nothing left for her here.

Except Sarah Lynn, she thought with a tiny smidgen of regret. Maybe the way the sun filtered through the pine trees early in the morning. And Caitlin. She would really miss Caitlin.

A tear shimmered on her lashes, then rolled down her cheek. Would she ever know the wonder of holding her own child in her arms? Even if she didn't, she would treasure the time she'd had with Taylor's daughter and consider herself blessed for having been part of Caitlin's life even for such a brief interval.

An uncontrollable sob rose in her throat. Damn Taylor for ruining it all! Why hadn't he been able to see that nothing in life mattered a hoot, unless there was someone with whom you could share it? Why hadn't he been able to trust her, to see that she would never, ever do anything to put him or his daughter at risk?

Well, it didn't matter anymore. She was tired of his misjudgments, tired of the way he refused to acknowledge his emotions, just plain tired of being the only one trying to make things work out. She would take her mother's treasured F. Scott Fitzgerald collection, the only thing in the house to which she was legally entitled, and go back to L.A. emotionally free, ready to find someone new and finally make a commitment that would last a lifetime.

She picked up the books and caressed the leather bindings and gold leaf lettering.

"Mama, I'm sorry," she whispered. "I'm sorry I couldn't do what you wanted, but I tried. I know what you wanted for me and I really tried."

Just then Sarah Lynn snatched open the screen door without even bothering to knock. "Hon, I think you'd better come with me."

"What is it? Has something happened to Taylor? Is it Caitlin?" she demanded as an irrational fear sent bile into her throat. Taylor and Caitlin were no longer her concern, she reminded herself sharply. She had to start remembering that. Knowing that didn't stop her blood from pumping faster.

"No, it's nothing like that," Sarah Lynn reassured her.

"What, then? I don't have time for guessing games. I'm trying to pack."

"Pack? To go where?"

"Back to Los Angeles."

"On Christmas Eve?"

"If I can finish this damned packing, yes."

"Well, it's just going to have to wait," Sarah Lynn insisted. "You're coming with me."

"Sarah Lynn, I am not budging from this room until you tell me what's going on."

"Jeez," Sarah Lynn muttered. "I'm not sure which of you has the harder head, you or Taylor."

"Leave Taylor out of this. I don't want to discuss him."

"Oh, really. Then why was he your first concern when I came running in here?"

"Will you just get to the point?"

"The point is that something's happening on the outskirts of town and I think you'd better see for yourself."

Zelda couldn't think of a single thing on the outskirts of town—or in the middle of town, for that matter—that she gave a damn about. Unfortunately she knew that Sarah Lynn matched her and Taylor for sheer bullheadedness. There would be no peace until she'd done what the woman asked. And there was the little matter of her own curiosity.

"Ten minutes," she warned. "I intend to be back here in ten minutes."

"Whatever," Sarah Lynn replied vaguely, dragging her off to her car.

The drive took less than five minutes, giving Zelda plenty of time to turn around and get back home within her limit...if she'd been able to budge once she got a good look at what had Sarah Lynn in such a dither.

"Oh, my God," she whispered softly as she stared up at the Port William water tower. Then she started to laugh, her heart lighter than it had been in months, maybe even years.

Taylor figured he'd gone and lost his mind. Better that, though, than his balance. He was perched precariously several hundred feet above the ground with a can of bright red paint clutched in one hand, a brush in the other.

He looked from the paint to the brush to his narrow perch and wondered how the devil Zelda had managed to splash her rude commentary on his parentage all over the side of this very same tower ten years ago without breaking her neck. For one thing, she must not have looked down. Every time he did, his head swam.

Having established that glancing toward the ground was very bad, he drew in a deep breath, dipped the brush in paint and began the message it had taken him too damned long to get around to sending. He just hoped it wasn't too late.

Red paint dribbled down from the hastily formed *T.* The rest of the letters in his name followed in an equally sloppy, though rather jaunty manner. He paused to admire the effect. Rather bold, if he did say so himself. One thing for certain, no one for miles around could miss it.

The distant sound of a siren told him that one person at least was aware of his highly illegal presence atop the water tower. He figured he had a very few minutes left in which to complete his task.

*L,* he began, then followed it with *OVES.* There was no time now to admire his handiwork. In the biggest letters he could manage without toppling from the narrow metal catwalk, he spelled out Zelda's name. So, there it was for all the world to see: Taylor Matthews Loves Zelda Lane.

"Taylor Matthews, have you lost your mind?" the sheriff shouted through a bullhorn. "You know you're defacing town property."

"And having the time of my life," Taylor called back, just as he sensed a vibration on the metal stairs up the side of the tower.

He glanced down and saw a familiar red-haired vixen climbing toward him. He tried to catch a good glimpse of her expression, but all he could tell for sure was that her brow was furrowed with concentration. Her knuckles might have been a little bit white as she clung to the railing for dear life.

He sat back, relaxed and waited. He figured no one, not the sheriff, not the mayor, not even his own father, would interfere in whatever drama was about to be played out high above the ground.

Finally Zelda reached the top rung and inched out onto the ledge. "I am too old for this," she murmured, sounding breathless.

Her cheeks were flushed. Wisps of hair curled damply around her face. Taylor thought she had never looked so beautiful, so desirable.

"Hey," he taunted, "where's your sense of adventure?"

"About five hundred feet below here," she retorted.

The look she cast him was almost shy. And hopeful, he decided. A good sign.

"Did you mean it?" she asked, gesturing toward the brightly painted words above them.

"Sugar, this is not the way to go about keeping a secret. Actually, I had more I wanted to say, but I ran out of room, and I was attracting a crowd."

"The sheriff is beginning to look a little apoplectic down there."

"How's my father taking it? I saw him drive up."

"He was reaching for his shotgun when your mother came along and told him she'd never forgive him if he did one single thing to interfere."

Taylor shuddered. "Thank goodness. He's a great shot."

"He probably would have aimed low," she told him dryly. "So what else were you planning to write up here?"

She'd tried hard to sound casual, but he could hear the uncertainty in her voice, an uncertainty that had never been there until he'd come along to shake her self-confidence. Taylor glanced over at her and waited until she'd turned to face him. He put down the nearly empty paint can and the brush, and took her hand in his.

"I was going to ask if you'd marry me," he said, searching her face for some clue about what her response would be. "I can't promise I'll change overnight, but I know that you're right. I haven't been living these past few years. I've been existing. It's way past time for that to change. I've missed you so much the past few weeks I could hardly bear it."

"I've been right here," she reminded him.

"But not with me."

She studied his expression with evident worry. "Taylor, are you sure? Really sure?"

"Never more so," he said adamantly. "It's time I got a grip on my life and did something to make it better, perfect in fact. Even Caitlin has pointed out that you're the best thing that ever happened to me. I was even thinking I might like a change of scenery, someplace to start over."

He could see the astonishment in her eyes and was glad he still had the capacity to surprise her.

"You'd move?" she said. "Where? Charleston? Columbia?"

Taylor shook his head. "I was thinking about Los Angeles. I know someone who already has some great contacts out there. What do you think?"

Her response was to scramble across the catwalk and fling her arms around his neck. Taylor wasn't sure if she was going to choke him or send the two of them crashing to their deaths. When her mouth slanted over his, he wasn't much sure he cared. It would be a hell of a way to go.

"Is that a yes?" he asked when he could speak again.

A grin spread across her face. "That is a definite, wholehearted yes." Her expression sobered, and she regarded him worriedly. "We don't have to go to L.A., though. We could stay here."

"No. I think two adventurous people such as ourselves belong where there's plenty of action, don't you?"

"Taylor Matthews, wherever you and I are, I promise you there will be plenty of action."

A little tremor of excitement washed through him. "If it weren't broad daylight and if there weren't a hundred people standing down there with their mouths hanging open in anticipation, I'd make you prove that right here and now. Since we can't, let's go down and share the news."

"Judging from the cheering, I think they've guessed," Zelda retorted as Taylor pulled her to her feet. "One last thing."

She took the brush and paint from him and while his heart filled to overflowing, she meticulously added one word to the sign: Ditto.

Yep, Taylor thought as they descended into the waiting arms of friends and the law. Life with Zelda Lane was going to be one grand and glorious adventure.

Her heart filled to overflowing, Zelda sat in Taylor's living room on Christmas morning. She was once again wearing the teal blue velvet skirt she had made from the material he'd given her. Caitlin was wearing her matching dress. Zelda watched with delight as Caitlin tore open her presents, exclaiming excitedly over each and every one, then running to hug whoever'd chosen it.

If Geraldine and Beau Matthews had been stunned to find Zelda here when they'd arrived, they were keeping their opinions to themselves. Beau hadn't mellowed exactly, but he hadn't made one single snide remark. In fact, thanks to Caitlin's exuberance, there hadn't been much time for conversation of any kind.

When she'd opened every last present, Caitlin sat back and announced, "This has been the very best Christmas I've ever had. Now, Daddy, you open your presents."

Taylor ripped off paper with as much enthusiasm as Caitlin had, saving the box from Zelda until last. When he opened Caitlin's gift to him, he hesitated for only a fraction of a second before proclaiming it the nicest shirt he'd ever received.

Then he picked up Zelda's package. Holding her breath, she watched him slowly untie the ribbon, then remove the paper with far more care than he had any of the others. Slowly, as if he was savoring the anticipation, he lifted the lid on the box. "A shirt," he said. "And two ties. They're..."

"Show us, Daddy," Caitlin demanded, shooting a conspiratorial look at Zelda.

Taylor held them up as if he weren't too certain what to make of them. Zelda winked at him.

"Fancy," Beau declared. "You'll look like a real Hollywood entertainment lawyer in that."

Taylor grinned. "What would you know about Hollywood entertainment lawyers, Dad?"

"I watch *L.A. Law*," his father retorted. "It's about time you stopped wearing those boring old white shirts."

Zelda, Geraldine Matthews and Taylor all stared at him in amazement.

"What?" he said. "I'm too old to know about what's in fashion for men?"

"Of course not, Dad," Taylor said. He gave the shirt one more slightly suspicious look, then said, "Okay, Zelda, your turn."

She picked up the package she knew Caitlin had wrapped. "Now what could this be? It weighs more than a butterfly."

Caitlin came and stood by her knee. "You can't give somebody a butterfly. Hurry up. Open it."

Zelda took her time with the package, to Caitlin's evident exasperation. When she unfolded the tissue paper inside, she found a lovely ceramic frame containing a portrait of Taylor and Caitlin.

"Oh, sweetheart, you couldn't have given me anything I'd have liked more."

Caitlin looked at Taylor. "See, I told you she'd like it."

"Of course I do. Why wouldn't I?"

Taylor regarded her ruefully. "She picked it out a month ago."

"Oh."

Geraldine Matthews handed over a silver-wrapped package then. "We have something for you, too."

Zelda's eyes widened. "You didn't need to get me anything."

"We wanted to give you this." She glanced around at her husband. "Didn't we, Beau?"

He nodded, his expression gruff, but no longer angry at finding her a part of their lives.

When Zelda had unwrapped the package, she found a delicate gold necklace inside with an antique locket. "It was my mother's," Geraldine Matthews told her. "She gave it to me on my wedding day and now I'm passing it on to you."

Zelda felt tears brimming in her eyes. She blinked them back. "Thank you. I'll treasure it."

"We just want you both to be happy. That's all we've always wanted for Taylor."

"Now mine," Taylor said, handing over a small package that looked suspiciously like a jewelry box. "Usually this is something that should be given in private, over candlelight, but I think we've pretty well dispensed with that tradition already."

Caitlin was so excited she reached over to help untie the ribbons. "I helped Daddy pick it out."

"Did you?" Zelda said, almost wishing she could delay opening the box for an eternity so she could treasure the joy she felt right this instant, the sweet shimmer of anticipation.

Unfortunately, Taylor was looking anxious and Caitlin was far too excited to be contained for long. She slowly lifted the lid on the velvet box. Inside was the most gorgeous diamond she had ever seen, surrounded by aquamarines.

"It's like your eyes," Caitlin told her.

"Not nearly so beautiful," Taylor corrected. "Not the way they're shining right now. You're not going to cry on me, are you?"

"I just might," she said.

"Does that mean you're happy?"

"Happier than I have ever been."

"Then you don't want to take back your acceptance of my proposal?"

She slid onto his lap and put her arms around his neck. "Taylor Matthews, you couldn't get rid of me now if you wanted to."

He grinned at her. "Then that makes this good for a lifetime," he said, sliding the ring on her finger.

Zelda glanced at his parents and saw that his mother had slipped her hand into Beau's. Tears were streaming down her cheeks, but she was smiling. Zelda knew then that nothing would interfere with her happiness again. For the first time in her life, she would have a real family.

She looked into Taylor's eyes. "I love you."

"And me?" Caitlin chimed in.

Zelda opened her arms to invite Caitlin into the embrace as well. "And you, darling."

"Have you picked a date for the wedding?" Mrs. Matthews asked.

"I was thinking New Year's Eve," Taylor said. "How does that suit you?"

"I couldn't think of a better way to start a new year," Zelda agreed.

"Not just a new year," he whispered as his lips claimed hers. "A whole new life."

\* \* \* \* \*

*Silhouette*

SPECIAL EDITION

*That*
SPECIAL
*Woman!*

## HARDHEARTED
### Bay Matthews

Chantal Robichaux would rather die than call on
Dylan Garvey again, but now she desperately needed
his help. Chantal's newborn baby—a baby Dylan
didn't know was his—had been kidnapped. If anyone
could find their son, it was tough cop Dylan. Dylan's
heart, on the other hand, would be hard to
reach...and only Chantal's love could soften
his defenses.

Share Chantal's loving reunion in Bay Matthews's
HARDHEARTED, available in January.

**THAT SPECIAL WOMAN!** She's friend, wife,
mother—she's you! And beside each Special Woman
stands a wonderfully *special* man. It's a celebration
of our heroines—and the men who become part
of their lives.

TSW194

# Take 4 bestselling love stories FREE

## Plus get a FREE surprise gift!

Share in the joys of finding happiness and exchanging the
ultimate gift—love—in full-length classic holiday
treasures by two bestselling authors

## JOAN HOHL
## EMILIE RICHARDS

Available in December at
your favorite retail outlet.

Only from  **Silhouette®**  where passion lives.

## Also available by popular author
## SHERRYL WOODS

### Silhouette Special Edition®

| | | | |
|---|---|---|---|
| #09595 | TEA AND DESTINY | $2.95 | ☐ |
| #09669 | MY DEAREST CAL | $3.25 | ☐ |
| #09713 | JOSHUA AND THE COWGIRL | $3.29 | ☐ |
| #09769 | *LOVE | $3.39 | ☐ |
| #09775 | *HONOR | $3.39 | ☐ |
| #09781 | *CHERISH | $3.39 | ☐ |
| #09823 | *KATE'S VOW | $3.50 | ☐ |
| | *Vows miniseries | | |

### Silhouette Desire®

| | | | |
|---|---|---|---|
| #05601 | NEXT TIME...FOREVER | $2.50 | ☐ |
| #05620 | FEVER PITCH | $2.50 | ☐ |
| #05708 | DREAM MENDER | $2.89 | ☐ |

(limited quantities available on certain titles)

| | | |
|---|---|---|
| **TOTAL AMOUNT** | $ | |
| **POSTAGE & HANDLING** | $ | |
| ($1.00 for one book, 50¢ for each additional) | | |
| **APPLICABLE TAXES**** | $ | _____ |
| **TOTAL PAYABLE** | $ | _____ |
| (Send check or money order—please do not send cash) | | |

To order, complete this form and send it, along with a check or money order for the total above, payable to Silhouette Books, to: **In the U.S.:** 3010 Walden Avenue, P.O. Box 9077, Buffalo, NY 14269-9077; **In Canada:** P.O. Box 636, Fort Erie, Ontario, L2A 5X3.

Name: _____

Address: _____ City: _____

State/Prov.: _____ Zip/Postal Code: _____

**New York residents remit applicable sales taxes.
Canadian residents remit applicable GST and provincial taxes.

SWBACK1

Silhouette ®